The Madwoman on a Pilgrimage

# The Madwoman on a Pilgrimage

Johann Wolfgang von Goethe

*Translated by*
*Jonathan Katz and Andrew Piper*

ET REMOTISSIMA PROPE

Hesperus Classics

Hesperus Classics
Published by Hesperus Press Limited
4 Rickett Street, London sw6 1ru
www.hesperuspress.com

First published in German in *Wilhelm Meisters Wanderjahre*, 1829
First published by Hesperus Press Limited, 2010

Introduction and English language translation, 'The Madwoman on a Pilgrimage'
© Andrew Piper, 2010
English language translations 'Not too Far!' and 'Who is the Traitor?'
© Jonathan Katz, 2010
Foreword © Lewis Crofts, 2010

Designed and typeset by Fraser Muggeridge studio
Printed in Jordan by Jordan National Press

ISBN: 978-1-84391-179-1

# CONTENTS

Illicit passions were nothing new to Goethe. At the age of seventy-nine, when the stories in this book were published, he had already chalked up a list of notable romances, consummated or otherwise. His first was with an innkeeper's daughter and others followed with an older married woman, a live-in mistress, and a girl fifty-five years his junior whom he pursued through Bohemia's spa towns. He married only once and that was to Christiane Vulpius after they had already been together for seventeen years and had a child. For the times, Goethe's approach to relationships and social order was hardly orthodox.

The three stories in this collection explore just such illicit passions, where social structures are jeopardised by untoward advances and unsuppressed longings: a father and son fall for the same mysterious woman; a young man rails against an arranged marriage; a mother's birthday is upset by the haunting passions of yesteryear. This isn't the Goethe we know from textbooks and grand theatrical productions. This is Goethe at his most irreverent, at his most unconventional.

The tales, 'Madwoman on a Pilgrimage', 'Who is the Traitor?', and 'Not too Far!', all date from the 1820s, the final years of Goethe's superlative output, when he had already long been the grandfather of German literature. Half a century earlier, as a young firebrand alongside Friedrich Schiller, Goethe had spearheaded a new wave of national writing, freeing it from the stiff collar of French-influenced courtly dramas and creating a string of Promethean characters who defied authority to pursue their passions, sometimes political, frequently sexual.

Indeed, it was one such character – and one such illicit passion – that made Goethe a household name. With his debut novel *The Sorrows of Young Werther* in 1774, Goethe introduced the world to a dashing hero in a yellow waistcoat who falls in love with the betrothed Charlotte. Werther pursues her until a stolen kiss leaves him with no choice but to take his own life using pistols borrowed from Charlotte's fiancé. The effect of this book cannot be underestimated. A blockbuster in its time, Goethe's debut set off 'Werther fever' across Europe, causing scores of jilted youths to don yellow waistcoats and indulge in copycat suicides like literary lemmings. Such was the power of an illicit passion.

But while *The Sorrows of Young Werther* heralded Goethe's precocious arrival on the scene, the stories presented here come from the writer's last novel, the sprawling work *Wilhem Meisters Wanderjahre*, published definitively just three years before his death at the age of eighty-two. The *Wanderjahre* (1821, revised 1829) is hard to categorise. It is a narrative gallimaufry where the travels of protagonist Wilhelm and his son Felix are interpolated with letters, poems, parables, aphorisms and, as some critics claimed unfairly, anything that was left on Goethe's desk in the twilight of his career. It is an unconventional book and these unconventional tales sit at its heart.

The father-and-son combo of Wilhelm and Felix pledge to spend no more than three days at any one place, keeping on the move, renouncing attachment and a bourgeois lifestyle. But Goethe knew that free-reined adventure without hurdle or constraint would interest neither storyteller nor reader. And it is passion's clash with order and attachment that is the crux of these stories, creating seemingly perfect parables for Wilhelm and Felix to digest on their travels.

However, these aren't the kinds of stories we are used to from Goethe. They don't read like parables. They don't point us towards haughty ideals or transcendental values. There are no Fausts, no Tassos, no Egmonts, no Werthers. Their teaching is elusive, perhaps non-existent. They are earthly tales of country folk: brothers, fathers, sons and sisters, all with the rumble of irreverent desire in their loins.

Here, we see Goethe with a mischievous glint in his eye. He teases the voyeur in us, pulling back the curtain for us to peek into a drawing room or a country inn as the sexual tension unravels. He invites us to watch as men who should know better are seized by their unrelenting desires, spurred on by a mystery woman wandering the road ('The Madwoman a Pilgrimage') or the spectre of an old flame ('Not too Far!').

But it is not enough just to watch. Goethe wants to draw us in. His denouements have a trace of malice, even sneering comedy, as the obsessed try to bury their passions with fragile excuses or wafer-thin decorum. We watch as protectors become seducers, husbands become adulterers, and the betrayers become the betrayed. These aren't the kind of characters that populated decades of Goethe's works. They aren't the descendants of Werther or Faust or Prometheus. They are not martyrs to their passions or victims of their fate. Rather, they are shifty, self-indulgent and exploitative. And, for that reason, they are all the more intriguing.

As a young man, Goethe subscribed to the ideas of his philosopher friend Johann Herder, who travelled across Germany documenting the bucolic bliss of country folk and their enchanting ways. But here, fifty years later, we see no trace of that Romantic vision. There is no place for the dignified ploughman, the honest milkmaid or the generous country lord. Here, Goethe's characters are manipulative, scheming, almost selfish.

In the first tale, 'The Madwoman on a Pilgrimage', we read of a mysterious yet graceful woman whom a baron discovers wandering a country road. Captivated by this lady of high birth with a shadowy past, the baron invites her to live at his family home where she becomes the focus of both his and his son's attentions. This story not only plays on the theme of attachment – central to the *Wanderjahre* – but also warps the relationships of father and son, beggar and benefactor, creating a near-farcical melodrama about who has overstepped the mark: the weird woman from the country road or the strait-laced landed gent? Even in 'Who is the Traitor?' – the most upbeat and playful of the three stories – Goethe's tone is ironic, almost disparaging. Ultimately, the happiness of the central couple is dependent on a series of deceptions and capricious partner-swapping, making us wonder how well-intentioned the cast of characters really is.

While these tales are riddled with improper passions, it would be wrong to say they are gaudy. Goethe refrains from daubing the paper with lascivious impropriety. Instead, he teases us with swipes at his characters and the reader; he implies 'secret unions' and 'fresh blooms [...] in pale cheeks' but never joins the dots. In the final tale 'Not too Far!' events turn on a man 'so passionately agitated by an apparently trivial incident'. Goethe knows better than most that a subtle turn of phrase can be more inculpatory than any snapshot of a couple in flagrante.

In 1963, the critic Richard Friedenthal called the *Wanderjahre* a 'repository for the wisdom of Goethe's old age'. If these stories are indeed the nuggets of a career dotted with its fair share of illicit passions, then we might conclude that we, too, are only a 'trivial incident' away from the maelstrom of our own illicit desires.

– *Lewis Crofts, 2010*

'Traitor!' Few words emerge more strikingly in Goethe's late work than that of '*Verrat*' or 'betrayal'. The three stories collected here are all drawn from a creative period in Goethe's life that began when he turned fifty and ended with his death at the age of eighty-two. They have been brought together because of their shared interest in this provocative nexus of erotic and communicative betrayal that became a hallmark of Goethe's later career. Whether it is the young pilgrimess who sings a tale of a miller's daughter betraying her lover to her family; the young man who betrays his true feelings about a mismatched fiancée; or the comical coach ride of 'Not too Far!' in which everyone betrays everyone else, infidelity was at the very heart of Goethe's thinking about literature towards the end of his life. As he would famously write in one of the poems accompanying his Oriental reverie, *The West-East Divan* (1816–17), 'Writing poetry is itself a betrayal.'

Infidelity in literature is of course an old topic, perhaps one of the oldest of topics. As long as men and women have been sleeping with each other, and then someone else, there have been tales to tell. But it was amidst the world of the early modern European court – and the genre of the courtly romance that it spawned – that infidelity assumed its most pivotal cultural role. Cross-dressing aristocrats hopping in and out of each other's beds and then lamenting their betrayals off in the woods or in a private changing room, this was the stuff of European literature for centuries, from Boccaccio's *Decameron* (*c.*1350) to María de Zayas' *Novelas amorosas y ejemplares* (1637) to Pierre Choderlos de Laclos' *Les liaisons dangereuses* (1782). The panoply of narrative infidelity – its seemingly inexhaustible supply of combinatory permutations

– provided early modern readers not only with an encyclopedic repertoire of cautionary tales but also that all-important ingredient of boundless readerly titillation. Like the unflaggingly horny lovers in their fictions, readers weren't supposed to stop either.

This is the world from which the heroine of our first story, 'The Madwoman on a Pilgrimage', emerges. She seems to walk literally right out of one of these courts and into Herr von Revanne's grove (suggestively called a *Lustwäldchen* in the German, a sexy little wooded space). He drops his book in surprise. At first we might surmise that, like Paolo and Francesca, no more will be read that day. But we would be wrong. She sighs and then he does too. *And then she goes home to work for him*. The dropped book is not a rather witless dirty joke, but a sign that something different is going on here. Something very different. We gradually learn that she looks like she belongs at court, but she is missing her retinue. There is something incomplete about her. She is surrounded by a vacancy, by something both we and the characters in the story cannot know. She is said to be on a pilgrimage, but we never learn her destination or her starting point. There is no Mecca or Jerusalem here, and not really much of God either. The circularity at the heart of the pilgrimage turns into a wandering, twisted line of secularity, a line that the reader cannot ultimately follow.

Perhaps no other story captured the two great fundamental transformations that were taking place in European societies at the end of the eighteenth century as succinctly and as comically as 'The Madwoman on a Pilgrimage'. In just a few short pages we symbolically experience the decline of both the aristocracy and Christianity *at the same time*. It is little wonder that it became a sensation in Goethe's circle in Weimar when it first appeared there – in its initial French version in the fateful year of 1789 – via Heinrich August Ottokar Reichard's *Cahier de Lecture*, a journal responsible for communicating all things French to German intellectuals across the Rhine. The arrival of the 'Madwoman' coincided, coincidentally or not, with the French Revolution that set all of Europe on its head. The story we have here is a translation by Goethe undertaken several decades later in preparation for his novel-cum-novella collection, *Wilhelm Meister's Travels* (1808–29). There was something about this story, and about the act of translation, that marked an important new point of departure for Goethe's late work. The madwoman or *Törin* was like a portal or *Tor* to the next phase of his career.

One of the essential ways that tales of betrayal had mattered to their courtly readers was through the dramatisation of a confessional moment. The act of erotic betrayal was often conflated with one of communicative betrayal as a jilted lover would recount the story usually alone in the woods or sequestered in a closet somewhere. But she or he was seldom alone: the story needed to be overheard by another party. The tale of betrayal, in other words, needed to be betrayed to someone else. Such scenes were a way for the narrative to argue for its own authenticity. Amidst all the flirtatious deceptions at court, there was still a space where individuals could disclose what they truly felt, where individuals could finally mean what they said. Such dramas of authenticity at the periphery were used to understand the dissimulation at the centre of the early modern court.

In 'The Madwoman on a Pilgrimage', by contrast, we never get this controlling framework. There is no stability at the margins any more. Betraying something (as opposed to betraying someone) is no longer framed as a guarantor of authenticity

– that this story is true because I do not mean to divulge it – but instead as a sign of a universal communicative malady. Things are constantly being betrayed to listeners, but we (and they) are never quite sure what. The pilgrimess sings a tale of a man who has been betrayed by his lover (she announces his presence early one morning to her family). At the end of the song the narrator tells us that this was the man who amorously betrayed her. After the song is over, the pilgrimess's listeners do not know how to respond. Is this 'romance' about her, especially when she is classified as a 'madwoman'? How can we be sure that a madwoman is telling the truth? And shouldn't we beware of making the elementary mistake of confusing a narrator with an author?

After the song is over we are told that her listeners were surprised that 'she could forget herself in this way'. Which self did she forget, the crazy one or the sane one? And yet such self-forgetting seems to be contagious. The listeners too, we are told, 'forget themselves', or at least what they said to her afterwards. In other words, no one has any idea what they are saying to each other any more. The pilgrimess seems to speak only in unintelligible aphorisms anyway, a modern-day sphinx. It is, in short, a world of pure misunderstanding, a point that reaches a fever pitch by the twist at the end of the story.

So why so much literary betrayal in this work that Goethe chose to translate and make the centre of his last monumental work of fiction? The simplest answer is that this was a translation and no association was more emphatic throughout the early modern period than that of the translator with the traitor. As the Italians had it, *traduttore traditore*, to translate is to betray, or as a popular group of French translators called themselves in the seventeenth century, *les belles infidèles*. Goethe chose this work to translate, one could say, because it was about the perils of translating and being translated, something that was occurring to him regularly as he became a star on the European literary stage. Like the listeners in the 'Madwoman', it was clear that Goethe's listeners in other languages very often had no idea what he was saying.

But on a deeper level, I think there is a more profound point to be made as to why Goethe was drawn to this element of communicative betrayal at the heart of translation in his late career. The schema that had surrounded tales of betrayal for centuries, 'court/simulation vs. not-court/truth', was giving way to a new universal truth of simulation at the end of the eighteenth century. According to this proto-modernist logic, all language games were simulations and thus all language games required interpretation, the filling in of the surplus of meaning that followed from the void of meaning at their heart, like the pilgrimess's missing retinue.

Such epochal shifts in how we think about language and literature were of course tied to major sociological changes, too. The tale of betrayal was a powerful way for Goethe to reflect on the changing nature of writing at the turn of the nineteenth century and the increasing distance between an author and his public. The courtly romance was predicated on the physical proximity of its interlocutors – that the means and the end were the same: one used one's body to communicate that one would like to use another person's body. Language was fundamentally gestural, and bodies were at the heart of interpreting the meaning of how we communicated with each other. But in a world that was increasingly mediated, in a world overwhelmingly shaped by writing, print, and the book, how was an author to retain control of the meaning of what he said amidst the swirl of so many distant and anonymous readers? How were these readers, disassociated from the personal connections to writers that had characterised the system of writerly patronage for centuries, to know what an author truly meant? It seemed that an unbridgeable gap had emerged, a gap that was at the heart of an increasingly mediated world.

If this sounds like it has a lot to do with our present, it does. That is one of the major reasons why Goethe still matters today. Few authors were as concerned with this change, with what it meant to inhabit a world suffused with written mediation, as he was. And few authors explored in more extravagant and thoughtful detail what it meant for us to inhabit this world than he did. I leave it up to readers to try and see how such fundamentally modern concerns with the treachery of written words also assume centre stage in the two other tales included here.

*– Andrew Piper, 2010*

# The Madwoman
# on a Pilgrimage

Herr von Revanne, a rich private citizen, owns the most beautiful lands in his province. With his son and sister he lives in an estate that is worthy of a prince. And indeed, with his park, his waters, his lease holdings, his manufacturing, and his own household supporting half of the inhabitants for six miles around, he is truly a prince through his esteem and the good that he engenders.

A few years ago he was strolling along the wall that accompanies the main road of his park when he decided to rest in a delightful little grove, a favourite spot of repose for travellers. The trees' lofty branches loomed over young thickets, as guests found shelter from wind and sun and a translucent spring directed its water over roots, rocks and grass. The wanderer carried with him book and musket as usual. He began to read and was pleasantly diverted and distracted by the songs of birds and occasionally by the steps of fellow travellers.

A beautiful morning was well under way when a woman, charming and youthful, strode towards him. She had left the road to seek the tranquillity and refreshment promised by the place where Herr von Revanne was seated. He was surprised; his book fell from his hands. The pilgrimess was endowed with the most beautiful eyes in the world and her face was enlivened by a delightful expressiveness. Her figure, her comportment, and her sense of decorum were all such that he involuntarily stood up and looked down the road to see the retinue that he supposed was following her. As she nobly bowed before him, his attention was once again drawn towards her figure and he honourably returned her greeting. The beautiful traveller sat at the edge of the spring without saying a word and then let forth a sigh.

What a strange power sympathy is! called out Herr von Revanne when he recounted this event to me. I responded to

3

this sigh. I remained standing without knowing what to do or say. My eyes were not sufficient to grasp such perfection. Lying there stretched out, leaning on her elbow, she was the most beautiful female figure that one could imagine. Her shoes gave me occasion to make a few observations. Covered in dust, they suggested a long journey and yet her silk stockings were so spotless that they seemed just to have been pressed. Her dress was not rumpled at all, her hair appeared freshly curled, fine lace, fine linen, she looked in fact as if she were dressed for a ball. Nothing about her indicated a journeywoman, and yet she was one, albeit a lamentable one and an admirable one.

Finally, I used the glances she directed my way as an opportunity to ask if she was travelling alone.

'Yes, sir,' she said, 'I am alone in the world.'

'What? Madame, you are without parents, without acquaintances?'

'That is not what I meant to say, sir. I have parents and plenty of acquaintances, but no friends.'

'In that,' I continued, 'you can undoubtedly bear none of the guilt. You have a beauty and certainly a heart that allows much to be forgiven.'

She felt the reproach that my compliment concealed and I immediately sensed her superior upbringing. She opened two heavenly eyes of the purest and most perfect blue in my direction, transparent and brilliant, at which point she said in the noblest of tones that she could not hold it against an honourable man, as I appeared to be, that he would be somewhat suspicious when he met a young woman alone on a road. It had happened to her repeatedly. But even though she was unknown, and even though no one had the right to interrogate her about this, she asked that I trust that the purpose of her trip was without doubt of the most honourable nature. There were causes that she did not need to recount to anyone but that necessitated bearing her sorrow throughout the world. She had discovered, she said, that the dangers that one feared for her sex were only imagined and that a woman's honour, even among highway robbers, was only endangered through the weakness of her heart and principles.

In addition, she only ever travelled at times and on routes where she felt secure, did not speak with just anyone, and resided periodically in decent homes where she could earn her livelihood through tasks for which she had been trained. At this point her voice sank, her eyelids closed and I saw a few tears fall from her cheeks.

I replied that I in no way doubted the goodness of her origins nor the admirable nature of her manners. I only regretted that some necessity forced her into servitude since she appeared so worthy of being served. I conveyed to her that I did not wish to question her further, despite a rather acute curiosity. Rather, I wished to convince myself, by getting to know her better, that she would indeed be provided for wherever she went because of her reputation and her virtue. These words appeared to injure her as she responded that she withheld names and places precisely for the sake of her reputation, which always seemed to contain in the end more supposition than fact. Were she to offer her services, she would provide testimony from the previous houses where she had worked. She would not conceal that she did not wish to be questioned about her fatherland or family. On this point she was absolutely certain and would leave her honesty and the innocence of her entire life up to heaven or her own word.

Expressions such as these did not allow one to suspect any madness on the part of the beautiful adventuress. Herr von

Revanne, who had trouble comprehending this decision to travel about the world, surmised that perhaps someone had wanted to marry her against her will. It then occurred to him that perhaps she felt a deep sense of despair caused by love. Miraculously, but also commonly enough, in the very moment that he imagined her love for someone else, he fell in love with her himself. He now feared that she might continue on her journey. He was unable to turn his eyes away from her beautiful countenance, which was illuminated by an enchanting, shadowy green light. If nymphs truly existed, no more beautiful one lay outstretched before him. The rather romantic nature of this encounter kindled an attraction that he was incapable of resisting.

Without thinking more on the matter, Herr von Revanne accompanies the beautiful stranger back to his estate. She puts up little resistance, he escorts her, and she shows herself to be familiar with polite society. She is brought refreshments, which she receives with graceful acknowledgment, but without artificial politeness. Awaiting the midday meal, she is shown the house. She remarks only on that which deserves mention, whether it is the furniture, paintings or the appropriate arrangement of a room. She discovers a library, knows the good books and speaks of them with taste and modesty. No idle chatter, no awkwardness. At table she has an equally noble and natural demeanour and a delightful conversational tone. Up to this point everything appears reasonable with her conversation, and her character is as charming as her person.

After the meal concludes a somewhat bold gesture makes her even more beautiful. Turning to Fräulein von Revanne with a smile, she says that it is her custom to repay a meal with some work, and as long as she is without money she likes to request a sewing needle from the hostess. Allow me, she added, to leave behind a flower on your embroidery frame so that in the future you will be reminded of the poor stranger when you look at it. Fräulein von Revanne replied that she was very sorry that she did not have any material ready and that she would have to forgo the pleasure of admiring her talent. At once the pilgrimess turned her eye to the piano. Then, she said, I will repay my debt in the currency of song, as was once the custom with travelling bards. She tested the instrument with one or two preludes that revealed a very talented hand. One no longer doubted that she was a young woman of high standing, endowed with a host of charming talents. At first her tune was lively and magnificent. Then she turned to more sombre tones, to the tones of deep-seated mourning, which one could immediately see in her eyes. Tears welled up in her eyes, her face changed, her fingers stopped. But then she surprised everyone as she began to perform a rather bawdy song accompanied by the most beautiful voice in the world, both cheerful and ludicrous. Since we later had cause to believe that this burlesque romance might have concerned her more intimately, I hope I will be forgiven for including it here.

*Where to with overcoat so briskly*
*When the day has barely broken?*
*Is our friend lamentably*
*To a pilgrimage awoken?*
*Who has robb'd him of hat and staff?*
*Freely does he go on barren foot?*
*Into the forest on whose behalf*
*Wild, snowy, and destitute?*

Queerly called from warmer games,
Where finer delights awaited,
How dreadful were the pilgrim's shame,
Had he not with overcoat alighted.
A rogue it was who him betrayed
And with his vestures departed:
Our poor friend alone conveyed,
Like Adam, naked and downhearted.

Why this way he went misguided
Towards that apple perilous of yore!
One who no doubt well presided
Within the miller's walls before.
This prank he will not well repeat;
From that house he stole away,
And once free amid retreat
Began in bitter tones to pray:

In her fiery glances read I
No syllable of her treason!
Seeming to enjoy love's prize,
Formulating such foul reason!
Could I in her arms but dream
How deceitful beat her breast?
Speedy Amour begged she to remain
And well obliged he our request.

To enjoy love's tender gifts,
Through a night that knew no end,
And then upon the morning's drift
A cry to mother did extend!
Thereon arrived a dozen kin,

A steady stream of folk came in!
Then came brothers, aunts and uncles,
There cousins stood and constables!

What a riot, what renown!
Each appeared a different creature.
Demanded from me blood and crown
Portrayed with awful feature.
Why insist you all, such lunacy,
Upon these gifts from our good youth!
You know that such rewards in truth
Require much diplomacy.

Amour knows to ply his trade
In timely style. No longer will
He than sixteen years abide
Flowers to bloom within a mill.
Hearing this they swiped my garments
But from them overcoat procured.
N'er have I such manifold affronts
In one single home endured.

Up sprang I and swore and cried,
Intent on passing through the crowd.
Once more the madwoman I spied
And oh, with beauty so endowed.
To my ferocity gave way
The mob with obloquy ensuing;
Thus to freedom made I my way
As from within the clan was stewing.

*Beware of ladies rustic or refined,*
*This should every man profess.*
*Leave to ladies of high mind*
*The right their servants to undress.*
*However practised in this art*
*No tender dues to us you owe.*
*Just change your lovers like your heart*
*But betray them not – think what you bestow.*

*So he sings in winter's hour*
*Nowhere a single sign of life.*
*I blithely laugh at his great strife*
*For fairly earned is fortune's power.*
*To every man it comes to pass*
*Whose mistress daily he misled,*
*And nightly too delinquently*
*To love's disloyal mill has sped.*

It was rather suspicious that she could forget herself in this way, and such inconsistency seemed to indicate an unbalanced mind. But, Herr von Revanne later told me, we too forgot ourselves, unable to offer a single reply. I have no idea how the spectacle concluded. The unspeakable grace with which she performed this farce must have captivated us. She pretended to be coy, but with a purpose. Her fingers completely obeyed her and her voice was enchanting. When she finished she appeared as composed as before, and we came to believe that she had only wanted to enliven the usual repose that followed dinner.

Soon she requested permission to be on her way. But at my nod my sister said that if she was not in a hurry and the accommodations did not displease her then it would be delightful to have her stay with us for a while. I thought of employment that I could offer her since she had indicated that it would indeed be a pleasure to remain with us. But on the first day, and indeed in the days to come, we only ever went on short outings to show her around. She never betrayed herself: she was endowed with reason and grace. Her mind was refined and perspicacious, her memory formidable, and her spirit so beautiful that it often aroused our admiration and focused our attention exclusively on her. She was familiar with the rules of decorum, and behaved so completely appropriately with each one of us, no less so with friends who paid us visits, that we were unable to reconcile her earlier eccentricity with her fine upbringing.

I no longer made offers to her to work for us in our home. My sister, who found her a reassuring companion, similarly saw to it to safeguard the stranger's sensitivity. They tended to the household duties together, and quite often the good child was reduced to working with her hands, although she was equally adept at all of the higher order tasks pertaining to any domestic economy.

In no time at all she had established a degree of order on our estate that we had never seen before. She was a highly judicious housekeeper and since she had begun to accompany us at table, she no longer removed herself out of a false sense of modesty but continued to eat with us instead without a second thought. Nevertheless, she never touched an instrument or cards until she had completed whatever task she had begun.

Now I have to confess that the fate of this young woman had begun to touch me deeply. I pitied the parents who very likely missed such a gracious daughter, and I lamented the fact that such tender virtue, so much uniqueness, should be lost to the world. For several months now she had lived with us, and

I began to hope that the confidence that we tried to convey to her would eventually bring that secret of hers to her lips. Were it misfortune, we could help; were it a misdeed, one would hope that our intercession, our testimony, would secure forgiveness for a passing error. But all of our assurances of friendship, even our pleading, were without effect. As soon as she noticed our intention to procure information from her, she would immediately hide behind some general maxims to justify herself without conveying anything to us. For example, when we spoke of her misfortune, she would reply: misfortune falls to the good and the bad. It is a potent remedy that strikes both the beneficial humours as well as the detrimental.

When we attempted to understand the causes of her flight from her paternal home she would reply smiling: the deer that flees is not the guilty one. When we asked if she had endured some sort of persecution: that is the fate of certain young women of noble birth – to experience and endure persecution. She who cries over an indignity will only encounter more. But how could she decide to entrust her life to the crudeness of strangers, or at least to depend upon their pity? To which she again laughed and said: the poor who greet the rich at table are not lacking in reason. Once, when the conversation was heading in a humorous direction, we spoke to her of lovers and asked if she knew the truculent hero of her romance? I am certain these words went straight through her. She opened a pair of eyes in my direction that were so austere and bitter that I could not endure her gaze. Whenever we spoke of love to her after that we could expect to see her graceful being and her lively spirit become clouded over. She would immediately fall into a state of mind that we supposed was brooding, but that was more likely a sign of pain. And yet in general she remained cheerful without too much vivacity, noble without

12

an air of prestige, direct without frankness, withdrawn without sheepishness, more patient than gentle, and more grateful than affectionate towards politeness and embraces. She was undoubtedly a woman educated for a great estate and yet she appeared no older than twenty-one.

So this young, inexplicable person, who had completely captivated me, appeared to us for the almost two years that she remained, until one day she committed an act of madness that was far more outlandish than her qualities were honourable and illustrious. My son, younger than I, will be able to console himself. I, for my part, fear that I am weak enough to miss her always.

I will now recount the tale of an act of madness of a sensible young woman to show that madness is often nothing more than reason in another guise. It is true that one will find a singular contradiction between the noble character of the pilgrimess and the rather farcical guile that she subsequently employed. But we are already aware of two of her other eccentricities, the pilgrimage and the song.

It is quite clear that Herr von Revanne was in love with the stranger. Admittedly, little did he wish to rely on his fifty-year-old looks, even though he appeared as fresh and vital as a thirty-year-old. But perhaps he had hoped to appeal to her through his pure, childlike health, through the goodness, cheerfulness, mildness and generosity of his character. Or perhaps through his property, although he was gentleman enough to know that one cannot buy what has no price.

The son, on the other hand, amiable, affectionate, fiery, and less considerate than his father, threw himself into the affair. Once she had become dear to him through his father's and aunt's praise, he tried to win over the unknown guest with delicacy at first. He honourably courted the charming young woman, who appeared to stoke his passion beyond reason. Her restraint inflamed him far more than her affections or her beauty. He ventured to persuade, to seduce, to make promises.

The father, without wishing it, endowed his entreaties with a rather fatherly air. He knew himself, and when he realised who his rival was, he hoped that he would not prevail through means that were unbecoming for a man of principle. Regardless, he pursued his course although it was no secret to him that material possessions, indeed even abundant amounts of property, were attractions that a young woman was drawn to not without some consideration and that were ineffective as soon as love encountered the allures of youth. Herr von Revanne committed additional errors that he later regretted. Amidst this honourable friendship he also spoke of the possibility of a long-term, secret yet legitimate relationship. He complained greatly and uttered the word ingratitude. Without doubt he did not understand the woman he loved when one day he remarked that many benefactors receive nothing in return for their goodness. To which she replied directly that many benefactors would gladly trade away all rights to their privileges for a lentil.

Entangled in the courtship of two rivals and driven into flight by unknown causes, the beautiful stranger resorted to a rather remarkable plan of escape from such precarious circumstances. It appeared that her aim was none other than to spare herself and others a series of foolish scenes. The son pressed with the audacity of youth and threatened, as is so often the case, to sacrifice his life for the implacable woman. The father, only somewhat less unreasonably, was equally solicitous. Both were honourable. This charming being could likely have assured her place in life – for both Revannes affirmed that their intentions were to marry her.

But let the pilgrimess be an example to all women that a decent soul, even if gone astray out of vanity or indeed madness, cannot bear the wounds of the heart that it does not choose to heal. The pilgrimess keenly felt that she had been driven to an extreme point where it would be difficult to defend herself for long. She was at the mercy of two lovers who could excuse every infringement through the purity of their intentions as they sought to justify their audacity through the thought of a celebratory union. So it was, and so she understood it to be.

She could have fortified herself behind Herr von Revanne's sister, but she did not, no doubt out of consideration and respect for her benefactors. She did not become unnerved. Instead, she devised a plan that would preserve everyone's virtue in so far as hers would be called into question. She was mad from fidelity, which her lover undoubtedly did not deserve were he not to see all of the sacrifices she had endured. It is doubtful he ever will.

One day, when Herr von Revanne responded with a little too much animation to the friendship and the gratitude that she showed him, she assumed a rather naive air that caught his attention.

'Your goodness, sir,' she said, 'worries me, and let me honourably divulge why. I am well aware that to you alone my entire gratitude is indebted, but admittedly –'

'Cruel woman!' cried Herr von Revanne. 'I understand what you mean. My son has touched your heart.'

'Oh! Sir, it did not stop there. I can only say in my confused state –'

'What? Mademoiselle, you would be –'

'I think so, yes,' she said as she bowed deeply and produced a tear. It is a well-known fact that women never want for tears during a performance and never lack an apology for their wrongs.

As in love as Herr von Revanne was, he admired with even greater fervour this latest display of innocent decency that emanated from beneath the motherly bonnet. He found her bow all too appropriate.

'But, Mademoiselle, this is incomprehensible for me –'

'For me, too,' she said, and her tears flowed with even greater vigour. They flowed for so long that Herr von Revanne, after a long and rather unpleasant reflection, resumed the conversation with a mild countenance and said, 'This clarifies everything! I now see how absurd my demands have been. I will not reproach you, and as the sole punishment for the pain that you have caused me, I will promise you as much as necessary from my son's inheritance to see if he loves you as much as I do.'

'Oh! Sir, spare me my innocence and say nothing of this to him.'

To demand discretion is not the means to achieve it. With these steps taken, the beautiful stranger expected to see her lover before long vexed and agitated approaching her. Soon enough he did with a look that promised devastating words to follow. And yet he faltered and could utter nothing more than, 'What? Mademoiselle, is it possible?'

'What do you mean, sir?' she said, with a smile that can drive a man to distraction on such occasions.

'What? What do you mean? Go on then, Mademoiselle, you are indeed beautiful! But at the very least one should not disinherit lawful children. It is enough to accuse them. Yes, Mademoiselle, I have seen through your plot with my father. You two are giving me a son, and it is undoubtedly my brother!'

With the same composed and cheerful visage she answered him, 'You are certain of nothing. It is neither your son, nor your brother. Boys are malicious. I do not want one. It is a poor girl whom I will bring away with me, far away, far from mankind, from the malicious, the fools, and the unfaithful.'

Upon which she continued, opening up her heart, 'Adieu! Adieu, dear Revanne! Nature has given you an honest heart. Maintain the principles of decency. They are not dangerous where there is much wealth. Be good to the poor. He who scorns the pleas of distressed innocence will one day plead and not be heard. He who is not considerate, considerate of the plight of a defenceless woman, will one day be the victim of inconsiderate women. He who does not feel what an honourable woman must feel when courted does not deserve her hand. He who forges schemes against all reason, against good intentions and against the plans of his family just to satisfy his desires deserves to forfeit the fruits of his passion and the respect of his family. I certainly believe you have loved me honourably. But, my dear Revanne, the cat is well aware for whom she licks her paws. Were you one day to become the lover of a deserving woman, you would do well to remember the unfaithful man of the mill. Learn from my example to trust the constancy and the discretion of your lover. You know whether I have been unfaithful, your father knows this too. I planned to travel the world and protect myself from all danger. Without doubt the dangers are greatest that threaten me here in this house. But because you are young, I will tell you this in confidence: men and women are only wilfully unfaithful. This is what I wanted to show my friend from the mill, who will perhaps see me again when his heart is pure enough to miss what he has lost.'

The young Revanne continued listening even after she had finished. He stood there, as though struck by lightning. Tears began to fill his eyes and in this state of calm he walked back to greet his aunt and his father, saying that Mademoiselle had gone away, Mademoiselle was an angel, or rather a demon, roaming the world and punishing every heart. The pilgrimess had made arrangements so that no one would find her. When father and son had unravelled her plot they no longer doubted her innocence, her talents, or her madness. No matter how hard Herr von Revanne tried, he was unable to uncover the slightest bit of information concerning this beautiful person who had appeared as fleeting and as dear as the angels.

# Who is the Traitor?

'No! No!' he cried, as he impetuously hurried into the bed-chamber allotted him and set down the lamp. 'No! It is not possible! But where am I to turn? Now for the first time my thoughts are at odds with his, for the first time my feelings, my wishes are other than his. Oh, Father, if only you could be here, invisible, if you could look right through me, you would see without any doubt that I am still the same, ever the true, obedient, loving son. But to say no! To fight against my own father's dearest, long-cherished wish! How can I speak out, how can I express this? No, I cannot marry Julie. Even to utter this thought aloud terrifies me; so how am I to stand before him and reveal it – to my good, dear father? I can picture him, staring at me in silent disbelief, shaking his head – that discerning, intelligent, learned man, lost for words. Alas for me! Oh, how well I know to whom I could open my heart and confide this pain, this perplexity, and whom I would choose for my advocate. Yes, it is none other than you, Lucinde – and to you I would first wish to say how I love you, how I give myself up to you, and then I would fervently implore you, "Plead for me, and if you can bring yourself to love me, if you would be mine, then plead for both of us!"'

To give an explanation for the passionate outpouring of this brief but heartfelt monologue will itself require rather more words.

Professor N… of N… had one son, a boy of striking beauty, whom he entrusted to the care of his wife until he reached his eighth year. She, the worthiest of women, guided the child's hours and days in living, learning and good behaviour in all he did. She died, and at that time the father felt that he was himself not competent to continue the task of caring for the boy. So far there had been complete agreement between the parents; they had worked towards one and the same end, they had decided together on what action was immediately necessary, and the mother was capable and prudent in discharging it. Now the widower's grief was doubled, indeed trebled; for he well knew, and saw clearly every day, that only by some miracle could the son of a professor acquire a satisfactory academy education. In his anxiety he turned to his friend the High Bailiff in R..., with whom earlier he had already talked over plans to strengthen their family ties. His friend was able to offer advice and help, and as a result the child was admitted to one of those excellent educational institutions that flourished in Germany at the time and where the utmost care was given to the whole person – body, soul and intellect.

And so now the son was well settled; the father, however, found himself all too alone – bereft of his wife and deprived of the sweet presence of that lad whom he had, through no great personal efforts, seen brought up just as he had desired. But here once again the friendship of the High Bailiff bore fruit; thanks to the very pleasure and diversion of movement and activity, the distance that lay between their homes soon disappeared; in a family that was, like his, without a mother, the bereaved young scholar now found two beautiful daughters growing up, both of them attractive in their own different ways. So it was that the two fathers now increasingly sustained themselves in the idea, indeed the expectation, that in days to come they would see their two households joined in the happiest of ways.

They lived in a prosperous principality, in which the capable Bailiff was assured of holding his position for life and probably also of being followed by a successor he would himself wish for. Now, in accordance with a judicious family and ministerial plan, it was intended that Lucidor be trained for the important post at present occupied by his future father-in-law;

and already he was proceeding step by step along this path. Every measure was being taken to impart to him the necessary knowledge, to give him the skills which the State always needs: attending both to the law of the land strictly imposed by the courts, and to that less stringent law, in the enactment of which intelligence and adroitness play a greater role; also accounting for the needs of the day, not excluding the more sophisticated financial matters, but all immediately relevant to real life, as would most certainly and inevitably be required.

With such considerations in mind Lucidor had completed his years of schooling, and he was now prepared by his father and his patron for the academy. He showed great talent in everything; and in addition Nature had rewarded him, through love for his father and respect for his friend, with the rare good fortune to be able to direct his gifts towards precisely those ends that they indicated – first out of obedience and later from personal conviction. He was sent to an academy abroad; there, according to both his own assessment in his letters home and the official reports of his teachers, he followed the very path that was to bring him to his intended goal. There was only one misgiving; in certain cases, it was said, he had shown himself too impatiently virtuous. Hearing this, father shook his head and High Bailiff nodded. Who would not have wished for such a son!

Meanwhile the two young daughters were growing up. Julie was the younger – mischievous, charming, capricious, highly entertaining; Lucinde was harder to characterise, as in her uprightness and purity she represented those very qualities that we find desirable in all women. The families paid each other visits in turns, and in the professor's house Julie found quite endless diversion.

Geography lay within the professor's special field, and was a subject he knew how to bring to life through topography. Just as soon as Julie had found a volume from the Homann series, of which there was a complete set, there would follow a survey of all the towns, critically examined and compared, some preferred, some rejected; any port met with her special favour, while other towns that were to earn even limited approval had to be distinguished by copious towers, domes and minarets.

Julie's father would leave her for weeks at a time with his proven friend; she really did advance in her knowledge and insight, and came to be quite well acquainted with the inhabited world in all of its principal characteristics and its most important locations. She was also most observant of the national dress of foreign lands, and if on occasion her foster-father playfully asked her whether perhaps one or another of those handsome young people that passed in front of the window might not appeal to her, she would answer, 'Yes, certainly, so long as he looks really unusual!' Now since our young students are far from neglectful of themselves in this regard, Julie not infrequently had occasion to notice, with interest, one or another of them who reminded her of some country's national dress. In the end, however, she would always insist that her minimum requirement was a Greek, decked out in full national apparel, if she were to devote her special attention to anyone; for this reason she longed to go to the Leipzig Fair, where one could find such figures on the streets.

After his dry and, at times, irksome duties, our instructor could find no happier moments than those spent playfully instructing Julie and inwardly triumphing at being able to educate such a charming daughter-in-law who was so unfailingly amused and amusing. The two fathers were, incidentally, quite in agreement that the young girls were to have no inkling of their intention, which was also kept secret from Lucidor.

Thus years passed, as they so easily do. Lucidor presented himself, fully accomplished and with all his exams passed even to the approval of his senior superiors, who wished for nothing other than the ability to fulfil with clear conscience the hopes of old and worthy servants, favoured and rightly deserving of favour.

And the matter had advanced in proper manner, and had at last come to the point where Lucidor, after his exemplary performance in some subordinate posts, was to accede to an advantageous position, which matched his proven merit and his aspirations and was situated precisely halfway between the academy and the High Bailiff's home.

The father now began to speak with his son about Julie as of his betrothed, his future spouse; thus far he had no more than hinted, but now there were no further doubts or conditions, and he extolled the good fortune by which his son had acquired such a jewel of a girl. In his imagination he saw his daughter-in-law with him again from time to time, busily occupied with maps, plans and pictures of cities; his son, for his part, remembered that most lovable, cheerful creature who had constantly delighted him with her playful teasing and friendliness. Now Lucidor was to ride over to the High Bailiff's home, consider more closely the beautiful and now mature young girl, and spend a few weeks with the whole household in order to deepen their mutual acquaintance. If the young people soon reached an agreement as was hoped, then word should be sent, and the father would appear without delay, so that through a solemn betrothal their longed-for joy might be secured once and for all.

Lucidor duly arrives, and is received in the friendliest manner. A room is assigned to him; he prepares himself, and appears. He finds before him, in addition to those family members with whom we are already acquainted, a half-grown son, a little spoilt but clever and good-hearted; if one were to accord him the clown's role, he fitted in well enough with the others. The household also included a quite elderly but hale and hearty and cheerful man, discreet, clever and refined, whose remaining purpose in life now seemed to consist in helping out a little wherever he could. Just after Lucidor there arrived another newcomer, a stranger, no longer young, of distinguished bearing, dignified and elegant, and highly entertaining by virtue of his acquaintance with the most distant parts of the world. They called him Antoni.

Julie's reception of her bridegroom-to-be was decorous but obliging, while Lucinde did the honours of the house just as Julie did her own. And so the day passed very agreeably for all, with the sole exception of Lucidor. He, reticent at the best of times, was now compelled to ask occasional questions in order not to lapse into complete silence; and in such a situation no one appears at his best.

Lucidor was thoroughly distracted; from the very first moment he had felt no dislike for Julie, no aversion, but simply estrangement. Lucinde, however, exerted such an attraction that he trembled when she looked at him with those full, pure, calm eyes.

It was in such affliction that he came to his bedchamber that first evening and poured out his thoughts in the monologue with which we began our tale. But to make sense of it, and to show how consistent is the vehemence of such floods of words with what we know already of the person, this will require a brief statement.

Lucidor was a person of deep sensibility, one whose mind was for the most part occupied with thoughts other than the immediate demands of the moment. For this reason he never enjoyed the greatest success in discourse and conversation; he was aware of this, and became taciturn except when the discussion turned to subjects that he had thoroughly studied, and for which he had the necessary knowledge at his finger-tips. What is more he had, first at school and later at the university, been deceived in friendships, having opened his heart with unhappy consequences; he was therefore suspicious of communication, and suspicion brings all true communication to an end. With his father, he was accustomed to speak only in agreement; he would therefore pour forth his brimming heart in monologues as soon as he was alone.

By the next morning he had regained his composure. But he very nearly lost it again completely when he encountered a still friendlier, warmer, freer Julie who had a host of questions for him about his travels by land and water, and how he had as a student walked and climbed his way through Switzerland with a pack on his back, even crossing the Alps. She wanted to know so much about that beautiful island in the great lake to the South; back then to the Rhine, she had to follow the river with him right from its source, first through the most disagreeable districts, then passing downstream through many a changing region until finally, between Mainz and Koblenz, the point comes where the river is still worthy to be discharged honourably from its last confinement and sent forth into the wide world and out into the sea.

This came as a great relief to Lucidor, and he now became the good and willing narrator, causing Julie to cry out, completely enchanted, that such sights should be savoured in company. And at this he was startled once again, for he thought he sensed in her words a suggestion of their journey together through life itself.

He was, however, soon released from his narrator's duties, for the stranger Antoni soon cast into the shadows all of those mountain springs and rock-faces and imprisoned and liberated rivers. The journeying now took them straight to Genoa, with Livorno not far away, and the most interesting sights of the countryside were merely snatched briefly in passing along the way. As for Naples, one simply had to see it before dying; but then of course there was still Constantinople – this too must not be missed! Antoni's decription of the wide world seized the imagination of all present, even if he himself had somewhat less fire to put into it. Julie was quite beside herself, and yet still far from fully satisfied; she still yearned for Alexandria, and Cairo, but above all the Pyramids, of which she had gained quite extensive acquaintance through the teaching of her father-in-law-to-be.

Lucidor that evening had hardly closed his door, had not yet set down his lamp, as he cried out, 'Now think carefully! This is serious! You have learnt, and thoroughly studied, much that was serious; but what does all that jurisprudence amount to if you cannot act justly right now? Consider yourself a representative, forget your own self-interest, and do what you would be obliged to do for another. This really is the most dreadful entanglement; that stranger must be here for Lucinde, and she is showing him the finest, noblest attentiveness of friendship and conviviality. The other foolish young creature would be only too willing to go straight out and travel the world with anyone at any time; and on top of it there's a real mischief about her – her interest in towns and countries is pure farce, just intended to silence us all. But why does this whole business seem to me so confused and complicated? Is the High

Bailiff not the most understanding, the most insightful, the most affectionate mediator? You must tell him how you feel and think, and he will at least understand your thoughts, if not your feelings. He can achieve anything with your father. And are the girls not both equally his daughters? So what does that Anton Wayfarer want with Lucinde, who was born to domesticity, to be happy and make others happy? What a delightful combination that would make – the bobbing quicksilver and the Wandering Jew together!'

Lucidor came down in the morning firmly determined to speak with the father; he would approach him without delay, during the hour when it was known he would be free. How great was his pain and perplexity to learn that the High Bailiff had gone away on business and was expected home only after two days! It appeared Julie was making this her travelling day too; she clung close to the World-Wayfarer, and abandoned Lucidor to Lucinde with a few light-hearted references to domesticity. So far our friend had seen the noble young girl only from a certain distance and had only a general impression of her, and yet he had already given his heart to her; now he was to learn, in the closest proximity, twice, nay three times as much as had already so drawn him generally to her.

The good old family friend, taking the place of the absent father, now came to the fore. He too had lived and loved; now, life having dealt him many a bruising blow, he was back at last at the side of the friend of his youth, refreshed and well cared for. He enlivened the conversation, and was particularly expansive on the subject of errors made in the choice of a life's partner; he had remarkable examples to relate of declarations both timely and belated. Lucinde shone forth in full splendour; she admitted frankly that in life the best possible results may come from chance happenings of every kind, and so it is in personal involvements; and yet how much more beautiful, she said, more uplifting, if a person could feel that it was to himself, and to the quiet, calm conviction of his own heart, to a noble resolve and swift decision, that he owed his happiness. There were tears in Lucidor's eyes as he approved these words, whereupon the ladies soon departed. The elderly gentleman who presided was more than happy to indulge in an exchange of stories, and so the conversation spread to amusing exemplary tales, which nevertheless so touched the inner feelings of our hero that only so refined a young man as he could restrain himself from bursting out; but he did indeed do so as soon he was alone.

'I contained myself!' he exclaimed. 'I must not grieve my good father with such bewilderment. I controlled myself, for in this worthy family friend I see the representative of both fathers. It is to him I will speak, to him I will reveal everything. He will mediate; indeed he has already nearly expressed my own desires. Surely he will not disapprove in the particular what he has found acceptable in general? Tomorrow morning I shall seek him out; I must have relief from this anguish!'

At breakfast the elderly gentleman made no appearance; he had, they said, spoken too much the previous evening, had sat up too long and drunk a few more drops of wine than was his wont. Much was said in praise of him, and indeed precisely such words and actions as drove Lucidor to despair that he had not turned to him immediately. This uncomfortable feeling was made all the more acute by his discovery that in such circumstances as these the good old man was sometimes not to be seen for a whole week.

A sojourn in the country has much to contribute to social intercourse, especially when those offering the hospitality are thinking, sensitive persons and have for years felt induced to come to the aid of the natural assets of their surroundings. Here, much had been happily achieved. The High Bailiff, first as a single man, then in the course of a long and happy marriage, had at his own expense, occupying as he did a well-remunerated post, followed his own vision and judgment, as well as the fancies of his wife and the wishes and caprices of his children; he had first arranged and nurtured separate plots both large and small, which when gradually and tastefully linked together by means of plantings and paths afforded those who wandered through them a delightful, changing and distinctive sequence of scenes. Just such a pilgrimage was embarked upon now by our guest at the behest of the family members; for there is always pleasure to be found in showing one's estate to a stranger, who may look with fresh attention on what to ourselves has become unremarkable, and the good impression he gains may stay with him forever.

The closer and the more distant surroundings were equally well suited to unpretentious arrangement, and indeed to some characteristic rural detail. Fruitful hillocks alternated with well-watered meadow-lands, so that now and again the whole scene lay open to view, without being flat. And while the land appeared to have been devoted first and foremost to utility, still there had been no neglect of charm and grace.

Next to the principal and adjunct buildings were situated pleasure-gardens, orchards and grass-gardens; emerging from these, one plunged suddenly into a little wood, through which wound hither and thither a broad, carriageable lane. Here in the middle, on the highest eminence, had been built a hall with attached chambers. On entering through the main door, one would see reflected in a great mirror the most favour-able view that the whole district could offer, and quickly one would turn back to recover, in the light of reality, from this unexpected vista; for the approach was most artfully arranged, and all was cleverly disguised so as to beguile and surprise. No one could enter here without turning repeatedly and delightedly from mirror to nature, and back from nature to mirror.

On that long and bright and most beautiful day, once on their way they made a thoughtful tour all over and around the whole estate. Here they marked the place where their good mother had often been in the evenings, where a glorious beech tree had commanded a clear space right around itself. A little further on, Julia playfully pointed out the place where Lucinde had practised her morning devotions, near a little stream running between poplars and alders, with meadows leading down and tilled fields rising up alongside. The beauty of it was quite indescribable! To be sure, one felt one had seen such things everywhere, but nowhere else had such sights been so impressive, so welcome in their sheer simplicity. In his turn the young squire also pointed, half against Julie's will, to the miniature arbours and childish little garden patches which, lying next to a cosily placed mill, were now hardly noticeable any more; these recalled the time when Julie, in around her tenth year, had taken it into her head to become a miller-maid, to run the mill herself after the two elderly folk had died, and find herself an honest young miller-lad.

'That was at a time,' exclaimed Julie, 'before I knew anything of towns on rivers, or even on the sea, nothing of Genoa and such places. It was your good father, Lucidor, who converted me; since then I haven't come here nearly so readily.' She sat down coquettishly on a little seat that scarcely held her now, beneath an elder bush that leaned too far down. 'Oh! Fancy crouching like this!' she cried, and leapt to her feet and ran on ahead with her lively brother.

The pair remaining behind conversed sensibly, and in these cases good sense draws closer to sentiment. Now they could discuss everything in detail as they wandered through that variety of simple gifts of nature, calmly contemplating how much an intelligent person of good sense can profit from these things, and how an insight into what lies right before us, when accompanied by a sense of what is needed, can work miracles, first in making the world inhabitable, then peopling it, and finally over-peopling it. Lucinde accounted for everything, and for all her modesty she could not conceal the fact that those commodious and pleasing connections between separate parts of the estate were the work of her own hand, under the direction and guidance or blessing of her revered mother.

But as even the longest of days must at last submit to evening, so their thoughts had to turn to their homeward journey, and as they pondered a pleasant, indirect route, the cheerful brother demanded that they take the shorter path, even though it might be less pleasurable and indeed more difficult. 'For,' he exclaimed, 'you have been making much of all your grounds and projects, and how you have beautified and enhanced the area for artistic eyes and sensitive hearts. But now allow me, too, to enjoy a little praise!'

Now they had to cross tilled fields and traverse rough paths, and even pick their way over stones scattered randomly and patches of marsh; then some way off they saw a great accumulation of machinery, towering up high in confusion. Viewed from closer at hand, it turned out that a large amusement- and pleasure-ground had been constructed, and not without judgment and a fair understanding of the popular demand. So here there stood, fixed at the appropriate distances apart, the giant wheel, on which the riders could remain seated horizontally and at ease as they went up and down, and other swings and swinging-ropes, see-saws, pleasure-rides and skittle-alleys, and everything one could think of to provide great numbers of people, on a large patch of common, with the most varied means of activity and entertainment. 'This,' exclaimed the young Junker, 'is my invention, my conception! And though father provided the money, and another clever fellow lent his brains, still without me – yes, the one you call the fool! – the skills and the money would never have been brought together.'

In such cheerful spirits all four arrived home as the sun set. Antoni presented himself; the young girl, however, who still had not had enough from this eventful day, had the horses harnessed and rode off across country to a friend, in utter despair at not having seen her in two days. The four who stayed behind felt all of a sudden at a loss, and it was even said explicitly that the father's absence was unsettling the party. Conversation was just beginning to flag when suddenly the jolly squire leapt up and quickly returned with a book, offering to give a reading. Lucinde could not resist asking how he had come upon this notion, which he had not had in a full year. To which he gaily answered, 'All my ideas come at the right time, and that's more than can be said for you!' He then read a succession of genuine fairy tales, of the kind that draw a person out of himself, play to his fancies and beguile him into forgetting all those restraints under which we find ourselves trapped even in our happiest moments.

'What can I do now?' cried Lucidor when he at last found himself alone. 'Time is pressing; I have no faith in Antoni – he is so unworldly, and I have no idea who he really is, how he came into this household, or what are his real intentions. He seems to care for Lucinde, so what can I hope to gain from him? All I can do now is approach Lucinde directly; she must know, and be the first to know. This was my first instinct; why do we allow ourselves to be diverted down clever sidetracks? The first thought shall now be the last, and I hope to attain my goal.'

On the Saturday morning Lucidor had dressed early and was pacing up and down in his room, considering and debating what he might say to Lucinde, when he became aware of a playful squabble outside the door, which presently fell open. A boy was pushed in by the jolly squire, with coffee and cakes for the guest. The squire himself bore cold food and wine. 'You should go ahead,' he shouted, 'for the guest must be served first; I am used to serving myself. My friend, today I am arriving somewhat early, and in commotion; let us enjoy our breakfast in peace, and then we shall see what to do, for we cannot hope for much from the assembled company. The little one is not yet back from her friend; those two have to be pouring out their hearts to each other at least once every fortnight if they're not going to burst. On Saturdays Lucinde is no use at all; she always presents the household accounts punctually to father. I was supposed to have a part in that too, but God protect me! If I know the cost of something, I can't enjoy a morsel of it. Guests are expected tomorrow, the old gentleman has still not regained his equilibrium, Antoni is out hunting, and we should be doing the same!'

Shotguns, pouches and dogs were ready prepared by the time they came to the yard, and soon they were away and off into the fields, where nothing more than a young hare and a poor, indifferent fowl were shot. Meanwhile the conversation was of domestic and current social relations. Antoni's name came up, and Lucidor was not slow to ask more about him. The jolly squire assured him, with a certain note of self-satisfaction, that he had already seen right through that odd fellow, no matter how mysterious he made himself. 'He is,' he went on, 'without a doubt the scion of a wealthy merchant household that fell to ruin just as he, in the fullness of his youth, was minded to embark upon great business ventures with all his strength and vivacity, and at the same time was to reap the many pleasures that were so plentifully on offer. Plunged from the pinnacle of his hopes, he picked himself up and, in serving others, he afforded them precisely what he could no longer achieve for himself and his own. He travelled the world, and acquainted himself with it and its reciprocal dealings in the minutest detail, while not in the meantime neglecting his own interests. Tireless activity and proven uprightness brought him, and preserved for him, unqualified trust from every side; everywhere he won acquaintances and friends, and it is indeed quite apparent that his wealth is just as widely distributed in the world as is his circle of acquaintances; for this reason his presence is needed from time to time in all four corners of the world.'

The jolly Junker's narration of this story was more circumstantial and naive, and included many droll observations, as if he were minded to spin out his tale to considerable length.

'How long he has been connected with my father! They think I see nothing, because I never meddle in anything; but I see so much the better – precisely because it is not my concern. He deposited a considerable sum with my father, who reinvested it safely and advantageously. Only yesterday he slipped a jewel-case into the old man's hands. I never saw anything more simple, more beautiful and priceless, though of course I only had a single glimpse of it, for it is being kept a secret. It is probably to be made over to his bride, for her joy and pleasure and future security. Antoni has placed his trust in

Lucinde. Still, when I see them together I cannot regard them as a well-matched couple. The other little tearaway would suit him better – and I also think she wants him more than the older girl does; she sometimes looks over at the old crosspatch so brightly and affectionately, as if she would any time happily leap straight into a carriage with him and fly away.' Lucidor controlled himself. He had no reply to offer; every word he had heard received his inward approval. The squire continued, 'In general the young girl has a perverse liking for old people; I really think she would as soon have married your father as she would the son.'

Lucidor followed his companion wherever he led him, over hedge and ditch; the two of them soon forgot about the hunting, which anyway promised little reward. They put up at a farmhouse where, being hospitably received, the one friend diverted himself in eating, drinking and chatting and the other lost himself in thoughts and reflections as to how he could turn his new-found knowledge to his own interest.

What with all these stories and revelations, Lucidor had gained such confidence in Antoni that he asked after him as soon as he entered the courtyard, and rushed into the garden, where Antoni was expected to be found. He hurried along all the paths in the park in the clear evening sun, but in vain. Nowhere was there a soul to be seen. Finally he passed through the doorway of the great hall. Strange to tell, the setting sun, reflected from the mirror, so dazzled him that he failed to recognise the two figures sitting together on the couch, though he could certainly make out that a woman was being ardently kissed on the hand by a man beside her. How great was his dismay to discover, as he regained his sight, Lucinde and Antoni there before his eyes. He would have liked the ground to swallow him up, but instead he stood rooted to the spot as

37

Lucinde, most amiably and uninhibitedly, bade him welcome, moved along, and asked him to sit down on her right. Involuntarily he sat himself down, and as she spoke to him, inquired after his day, and begged forgiveness for her absence through domestic duties, he could scarcely bear hearing her voice. Antoni stood up and took his leave of Lucinde; she, also rising to her feet, invited Lucidor, who remained, to go for a walk. Walking at her side he was reserved and self-conscious; she too seemed disturbed, and if Lucidor had been even a little aware of himself he would have gathered, from her deep breathing, that she was trying to hide heartfelt sighs. She finally took her leave as they neared the house, but Lucidor turned, at first slowly and then more impetuously, back towards the open country. The park was too constricting for him, and so he headed off through fields, hearing only the voice of his heart and wholly unaware of the beauties of that incomparable evening. As soon as he was alone with himself and able to give vent to his feelings in a comforting outpouring of tears, he cried out, 'A few times already in my life, but never so cruelly, I have felt the pain that makes me now so utterly miserable: when the happiness we have most dearly desired at last takes us by the hand, opens its arms to us, and at that very moment declares its parting for ever. I sat beside her, walked along close to her, her dress brushing against me in its movement, and I had already lost her! But do not dwell on it, do not torture yourself with it; be silent, and be resolved!'

He had forbidden himself to speak further; silent, pensive, he journeyed on through fields, meadows and thickets, not always choosing the most passable of tracks. Only when he arrived, late, in his room, he could no longer contain himself and cried out, 'Tomorrow morning I shall depart; never again can I endure such a day!'

And so he threw himself, fully clothed, on the bed. He was soon asleep: such is the happy, healthy lot of youth! The tiring day's activity had earned him the sweetest rest at night. But he was roused from the comfort of his morning dreams by the very first sunlight; it was indeed the longest day in the year, and threatened to be far too long. If he had been unable to feel the grace of the gentle evening star, now the exhilarating beauty of morning brought him only to despair. The world was, he saw, as beautiful as ever; so it was to his eyes, but his inner self dissented, for none of this belonged any more to him, now he had lost Lucinde.

His travelling-bag, which he intended to leave behind, was packed quickly. He left no note; his absence from the family table, and perhaps in the evening too, was to be excused with but a few words by the groom, whom in any case he had to wake. But he found the groom already down below before the stables, striding up and down. 'You surely don't wish to ride now?' exclaimed the normally good-natured fellow with some annoyance. 'I'm sure I can be frank with you – the young gentleman is becoming more insufferable by the day. Was he not gallivanting about in the area yesterday, so that one might think he would thank God for a rest on a Sunday morning? But no, he appears first thing, goes crashing about in the stables, and when I leap out of bed he saddles and bridles your horse. I can't hold him back for the life of me; he swings himself up and shouts out, "Just think what a fine deed I'm doing! This creature only ever goes calmly along at a well-considered judicious trot, but I'll see to it that he's roused to a lively gallop!" That is pretty well what he said, plus a few other strange things.'

Lucidor was doubly, indeed trebly dismayed, for he loved this horse precisely because it so matched his own character and mode of life, and he resented seeing the good, under-standing creature in the hands of a reckless hothead. Further-more his plan had been frustrated, his intention to flee in this crisis to a university companion with whom he had lived to-gether in a good, close friendship. That former trust had been reawakened; he thought nothing of the miles that separated them, and he had fancied he was already receiving advice and support from this benevolent and discerning comrade. This prospect was now excluded – but perhaps not after all, if he ventured to achieve his goal on his own sturdy feet, which now stood ready at his command. His first aim now was to be out of the park, into the open fields and onto the path that would take him to his friend. He was not quite sure of his direction, but at that moment, to his left, he caught sight of the peculiar edifice of the hermitage, which had previously been kept a secret from him; and, much to his astonishment, he espied there on the balcony beneath the Chinese-style roof the good old gentleman who for several days had been supposed ill, now cheerfully looking around. The most cordial of greetings, and a pressing invitation to come up and join him, were met by Lucidor with excuses and gestures of haste. It was only out of sympathy for the good old man, who tottered hurriedly down the steep steps and threatened to tumble all the way down, that Lucidor could bring him-self to approach him, and then allow himself to be ushered up. He stepped with astonishment into the charming little room; it had only three windows, facing the grounds, a most enchanting outlook, and the other walls were adorned, or rather completely covered, with hundreds of portraits, some being copper-engravings, some of them drawings, fixed to the wall next to each other in a certain order and separated by coloured surrounds and spaces.

'You are indeed favoured, my friend, as none other would be; this is the holy of holies in which I am happily whiling away my remaining days. This is where I recover from all those mistakes that society has led me to make, and here I bring myself back into balance after my dietary lapses.'

Lucidor surveyed the whole scene and, being himself well informed in history, he quickly discerned an underlying historical design in the arrangement. 'Up here in the frieze,' said the old man, 'you can find the names of distinguished men of antiquity, and others also from later times, again only the names, because it would be difficult to discover how they really looked. But here, in this main area, this is where my lifetime really starts; here are the men whose names I was still hearing as a boy. For around fifty years is the lifetime of the names of eminent people in common memory – after that the names either wholly disappear or become legends. My parents were German, but I was born in Holland, and for me William of Orange, as Regent and as King of England, is the forefather of all exceptional men and heroes.

'But here you can see Louis XIV right next to him. He it was who…' How gladly would Lucidor have interrupted the good old fellow, had this been as opportune for him as it is for us as narrators of the tale! For he felt under the imminent threat of recent history, indeed right up to the most recent, as was clearly to be seen when he glanced at the pictures of Frederick the Great and his generals. To be sure, the kindly young man respected the lively interest the old man took in his own times and those that just preceded his lifetime, and the fascination of particular individual views and characteristics could not escape him; nevertheless, he had already heard this recent and very recent history at his academies, and what we have heard once we tend to think we know forever. His thoughts were far away; he heard not a word, and he hardly saw anything either. He was just on the point of bursting out of the door in the most unseemly way and crashing down the long, lethal staircase, when a clap of hands was heard, loud and clear, from down below.

As Lucidor held back, the old man put his head out the window, and a familiar voice rang out from down below: 'Come down, for Heaven's sake, from your historical picture gallery, Sir! Cease your fasting, and help me to appease our young friend when he discovers the truth! I handled Lucidor's horse a little roughly, and it has lost a shoe. I've had to leave it standing. What will he say? It's just too absurd, when people are so absurd!'

'Come up!' said the old man, and turned back to Lucidor: 'Well, what do you say?' Lucidor was silent, and the wild young squire stepped inside. The exchange of words became a long scene; briefly stated, a decision was taken that the groom be sent immediately to take care of the horse.

Leaving the old man behind, the two youngsters hurried to the house, to which Lucidor was not wholly unwilling to be drawn; come what may, at least within these walls was contained his heart's one desire. When we are in such despair, our free will anyway tends to forsake us, and we feel momentarily relieved by the intervention of certainty and necessity from some quarter. Nevertheless, Lucidor found himself, on re-entering his room, in a very strange state of mind, rather like someone involuntarily forced to return to a room at an inn which he has just left, because an axle has broken.

The jolly young squire went straight for his travelling-bag, and set about unpacking everything in a most orderly manner; he gave particular attention to what he had in the way of more formal clothing, even if this was a part of his travelling

42

wardrobe. He pressed Lucidor to put on shoes and stockings; he ordered his copious brown curly locks for him, and dressed him up most handsomely. Then he exclaimed, as he stood back and inspected our friend and his own efforts, 'Now, sir, young friend, you do look like one who could stake a claim to pretty young girls and, what is more, serious enough to be looking around for a bride! Now just one moment, and you shall see that I too know how to present myself when the hour strikes. I learnt this from officers, at whom the girls are always looking out of the corners of their eyes; and I have myself enrolled in a certain troupe, so now they look at me too, and they may take a second look, because none of these girls knows what to make of me. This looking and re-looking, this awe and attentiveness, often yields something rather special, and even if it may not last it is still worth considering for a moment!

'But now come, friend, and do me the same service. When you see me slip, piece by piece, into my apparel, you will not deny that there's some wit and inventiveness in this fickle young fellow.'

He now dragged his friend off with him, through the rambling passageways of the old mansion.

'I have made my nest deep down at the back,' he proclaimed. 'Not that I want to hide myself away, but I like being alone: for it's hard to get things right with other people.'

They were passing the chancellery just as a servant stepped out with a writing-box of the old style, black, large and complete, including the paper.

'You don't have to tell me what's going to be written down there amongst the blots,' said the squire. 'Off you go, and leave the key with me! Just take a look in there, Lucidor. That will keep you out of mischief until I am dressed. A friend of the law won't find such a locality as hateful as would a man of the stables.' And with these words he thrust Lucidor into the courtroom.

The young man immediately felt he was in a familiar, friendly element, recalling those days when, devoted to his work, he used to sit at just such a table and practise listening and writing. Nor did it escape him that the room in which he now sat was a fine former house chapel now converted, in accordance with the changes in religious allegiances, to the service of Themis. In the book-presses he found subject headings and records already familiar to him; he had himself worked on these very proceedings, he remembered, in the capital. Opening one bundle, he came upon a document in fair copy which he personally had transcribed, and another of which he had himself been the author. Handwriting, paper, chancellery seal and presiding magistrate's signature – all of it brought back to him that earlier time of upright endeavour and youthful aspiration. And when he looked around and noticed the High Bailiff's seat, the seat destined and held for him, so fine a position, so worthy a sphere of work, and yet one which he was now in danger of spurning and renouncing, all of this doubly and trebly oppressed him, while at the same time Lucinde's form seemed to grow more distant from him.

He wanted to go out into the open air, but found himself a prisoner. His odd companion, being either thoughtless or mischievous, had locked the door behind him, but our friend was not left for long in this most painful constriction, for the other returned, excused himself, and through his eccentric presence inspired genuine good humour. A certain boldness in the colours and cut of his clothing was tempered by an innate taste, rather as we cannot refuse a degree of approval even for tattooed Indians. 'Today,' he piped up, 'shall make up for all of the boredom of these last days; good friends, lively friends, have come, pretty girls, merry young creatures in love, and then also my father – and, wonder upon wonder, yours too! It is going to be such a celebration; everybody is already assembled in the hall at breakfast.'

Lucidor felt, all of a sudden, as if he were staring into a deep fog; all the guests, known and unknown, were mere wraiths to him. Still his character, accompanied by a pure heart, sustained him, and after just a few seconds he felt he was a match for anything. Now, as his friend hurried along, he followed him with surer footing, firmly resolved to see things through, whatever might happen; he would declare himself, whatever the consequences.

And yet he was discomfited on the very threshold of the hall. In the large semicircle around the windows his eye fell immediately on his father, together with the High Bailiff, both of them ceremonially dressed. The sisters, Antoni, and some other familiar and unfamiliar persons he quickly surveyed at a single glance, which was on the point of clouding over. Hesitantly he approached his father, who bade him welcome in the friendliest terms, though with a certain formality that hardly encouraged any sharing of confidences. Standing before such an assembly, he looked about for a moment for an appropriate place for himself; he could have positioned himself next to Lucinde, but Julie, having little taste for stiff decorum, turned in such a way that he had to join her; Antoni remained next to Lucinde.

At this crucial moment Lucidor felt like one under a commission and, fortified by all his legal expertise, he brought into play, in his own interest, that excellent maxim, 'We should discharge those dealings entrusted us by strangers as if they were our own; why, then, should we not discharge our own

45

dealings likewise?' Being well practised in public delivery, his mind quickly ran through what he had to say. The assembled company had meanwhile grouped into a semicircle, and seemed to be outflanking him. He certainly knew what was to be the drift of his speech, but the correct opening eluded him. At that point he noticed, upon a table in a corner, the great inkwell, with chancery employees standing by. The High Bailiff made a movement to start his speech; Lucidor wanted to pre-empt him, and at this very moment Julie squeezed his hand. Whereupon he quite lost his self-composure, convinced that all was now decided, and all was lost.

There was now nothing more to be said for simply up-holding the present state of affairs and preserving family ties and the niceties of social propriety; he stared straight ahead, withdrew his hand from Julie's, and was so quickly out of the door that he was gone from the company's sight before they even realised it – and indeed he himself, now outside, felt wholly disoriented.

Shy of the daylight which now blazed down on him with full force, shunning the attention of people he met with, fearful of those who might come searching for him, he strode out and presently came to the garden house. There his knees were about to fail him; hurtling in, he threw himself inconsolably on the sofa under the mirror. To have fallen victim, in the midst of that respectable and proper company, to such confusion, which pounded to and fro like a wave inside him! His former self was at war with the present; it was indeed a dreadful moment.

And so he lay a while, his face sunk in the cushion on which just yesterday Lucinde's arm had rested. Utterly submerged in his pain, he suddenly leapt to his feet at the sensation of being touched, without having felt the approach of any other person, and there he saw Lucinde standing beside him.

Assuming that they had sent her to call him back, and had instructed her to use the appropriate sisterly words to return him to their company and confront his awful fate, he cried out, 'It is not you that should have been sent, Lucinde, for you are the very one that drove me from that place! I will not return! If you have any pity within your heart, kindly grant me the opportunity and the means to escape. And so that you may be able to attest how impossible it was to bring me back, take now the key to my behaviour, which must seem deranged, to you and to everyone. Hear the oath which I swore within myself, and which I now repeat aloud, indissolubly: only with you would I wish to live, to spend and to enjoy my youth, and so also live out a most true and honest old age. And let this oath which I now swear be just as firm and certain as any oath that ever was sworn at the altar, as I, the most pitiable of all mankind, take my leave of you.'

He made a movement as if to slip past her, who stood so close before him; but she gently caught him in her arms. 'What are you doing?' he cried.

'Lucidor,' she cried back, 'you have no need to be pitied as you believe. You are mine, and I am yours. I have you in my arms; fear not to put yours around me! Your father is entirely happy; Antoni is to marry my sister.'

Astonished, he drew back from her. 'Can this be true?'

Lucinde smiled and nodded, and he freed himself from her arms.

'Allow me to see just once more from a distance what is to be so close to me, most closely mine!' He clasped her hands, and they looked into each other's eyes. 'Lucinde, are you really mine?'

She answered, 'Yes, yes, I am.' And the sweetest tears came to those truest of eyes. He embraced her, placed his head next

47

to hers, and clung like a shipwrecked man to a rock; the ground still heaved beneath his feet, but now his enchanted eyes, opening again, fell upon the mirror. There he saw her in his own arms, himself enveloped in hers; he gazed again and again at the scene. Such emotions stay with a person life-long. At the same time he saw, reflected on the mirror's surface, that landscape which yesterday had seemed so grim and ominous, now more radiant and lovely than ever; and himself in such a position, on such a background! Sufficient reward indeed for all the pains he had endured.

'We are not alone,' said Lucinde, and hardly had he recovered from his enchantment when young girls and boys appeared, all festively dressed and garlanded, carrying wreaths and blocking the way out. 'All of this was supposed to be quite different,' Lucinde exclaimed. 'It was arranged so beautifully, yet now all is in such disarray!' A spirited march sounded forth from a distance, and the company was seen advancing on the broad roadway, festive and merry. He hesitated to go out to them, and seemed unsure of his footing unless she held him; she remained by his side, awaiting from moment to moment the solemn event of reunion, and of thanks for a forgiveness already granted.

And yet the capricious gods had decreed otherwise; a postilion's merry horn-blast sounded from the other direction, and seemed to throw the whole company into confusion. 'Who could be coming?' cried Lucinde. Lucidor shuddered at the prospect of a stranger arriving, and to be sure the carriage seemed quite unfamiliar. A two-seater, new, indeed the latest mode of conveyance! It drove right up to the building. A fine, well-bred youngster jumped down from the back and opened the carriage door, but no one came out; the vehicle was empty. The lad himself climbed in, and with a few skilful movements of the hand he threw back the top covering; in an instant all those who had now arrived saw ready before their eyes the most delightful contrivance ever designed for the most pleasurable of excursions. Antoni, hurrying ahead of the rest, escorted Julie to the carriage. 'Just try,' he said, 'and see if this vehicle may be to your liking, that you may journey through the world with me on the finest roads – for I will take you on no others – and wherever there is any need we will know how to make do for ourselves. Over the mountains we shall be carried by packhorses, and the carriage along with us.'

'You are quite the dearest of creatures!' cried Julie. The boy stepped forward and showed, with the deftness of a conjurer, all the conveniences, the little appliances and clever devices that the little carriage had to offer.

'I can think of no way on earth to thank you,' said Julie. 'Only on this little moving paradise, from this cloud into which you lift me, will I thank you from the bottom of my heart.' She had already leapt in, affectionately casting him a glance and blowing a kiss. 'For the present you may not come in with me, but there is one other whom I will take with me on this trial journey; he still has another trial to endure.' She called Lucidor who, being at that moment engaged as a silent partner in conversation with his father and father-in-law, was glad enough to be forced into the little carriage, since he felt an inescapable need to divert himself somehow, even for a brief moment. He took his place next to her, and she called out to the driver which way he should go. In an instant they were away, shrouded in dust, out of sight of the astonished onlookers.

Julie settled herself securely and comfortably into the corner. 'Now you move into that corner, my brother-in-law, so that we may look at each other quite comfortably eye to eye.'

LUCIDOR: You sense my perplexity, my embarrassment. I am still as if in a dream; you must help me out of it.

JULIE: See these charming country people, how they greet us so graciously. While you have been here you have not yet gone to the upper village. They are all thriving people, and kindly disposed towards me. But no one is so well off that you may never do him some significant kind service. This road, on which we now ride so easily, was laid by my father – this too was one of the benefits he brought.

LUCIDOR: I can well believe it, and I acknowledge it. But what are these external matters, compared with the turmoil within me?

JULIE: Just be patient; I will show you the kingdoms of the world in all their splendour. Now here we are at the top! See how clear the land lies against the mountains! All these villages owe so much to my father, and perhaps also to my mother, and their daughters too. Right up to the green of that little town over there, that is how far our land stretches.

LUCIDOR: I find you in a strange mood; you seem not to be saying quite what you would wish to say.

JULIE: Now look down here to the left; see how beautifully everything takes shape before us! The church with its tall lime-trees, the residence and its poplars behind the village hillock. And over there are the gardens and the park.

The carriage had picked up speed.

JULIE: You know that building over there; it looks just as fine from here as the surrounding country does from there. We shall stop here, by this tree; now, just at this point we are being reflected up in the great glass and are seen quite clearly from there, though we cannot see ourselves. – Drive on! – I do believe, a little while ago, two persons looked upon themselves in that mirror and, if I am not much mistaken, to their great mutual contentment!

Lucidor, irked at this, gave no reply. They journeyed on for a time, both of them in silence as they sped along. 'Here,' said Julie, 'is where the bad road begins. Here's a good turn for you to do some day. Before we start going down, look over there; my mother's beech tree dominates everything with its glorious regal head. You go on now,' she continued to the coachman, 'on the rough road, while we take the footpath through the valley, and we'll be over there before you.' As she stepped down she called, 'You'll have to admit it; that Wandering Jew, the restless Roaming Anton, knows how to arrange his pilgrimages comfortably enough both for himself and his companions; this is a very fine, comfortable carriage.'

And now she was already at the bottom of the hill; Lucidor followed, deep in thought, and found her sitting on a well-placed bench, which was Lucinde's own little spot. She called him over to join her.

JULIE: Now we sit here together, and are nothing to each other; so that is just how it had to be. The little Miss Quicksilver did not appeal to you. Love for such a creature was impossible; you could not bear her.

Lucidor's astonishment grew.

JULIE: But Lucinde! Ah, she is the very essence of every perfection, while the charming younger sister quite simply had no hope at all! But I see it; on your lips hangs the question: who was it that informed us so accurately?

LUCIDOR: There is some treachery behind this!

JULIE: Indeed! There is a traitor in the story.

LUCIDOR: Name him.

JULIE: He is soon exposed. It is yourself! You have the habit – laudable or unlaudable – of talking to yourself, and I must confess in the name of all of us, we have listened to you in turns.

LUCIDOR (leaping to his feet): A fine kind of hospitality that is, setting such a trap for strangers!

JULIE: Not at all! We had no thought of eavesdropping, no more on you than any other. You know how your bed is in a recess in the wall; on the other side of that wall is another alcove, which normally serves as a household repository. A few days earlier we had made our old friend sleep there, since we were much concerned for him in his isolated retreat; and then right on the first evening you plunged into a soliloquy of such passion, the content of which he revealed to us at the first opportunity the next morning.

Lucidor had no wish to interrupt. He drew away from her.

JULIE (getting to her feet and following him): What a great service this revelation did for us! I will happily admit that, while I did not find you exactly repellent, the circumstances that lay in store for me were far from desirable. To be Mrs High Bailiff – what a terrible fate! To have an excellent, virtuous husband who is to pronounce justice to the people, and for sheer justice cannot see his way to being really just, who cannot truly do those due justice who stand above or below him, or for that matter – and this is the worst of it – even himself! I know what my mother endured through my father's adamantine incorruptibility. At long last, sadly after her death, he developed a certain mildness, and seemed to be making himself a little more at home in the world and accommodating himself to it, having up till then struggled in vain against it.

LUCIDOR (highly dissatisfied at the situation, and indignant at the light-heartedness of Julie's treatment of him, stood still): As sport for one evening there was perhaps a place for this, but to perpetrate such mortifying deception on an innocent guest, day after day, this is not pardonable.

JULIE: We were all partly guilty; all of us eavesdropped. But I alone am atoning for the guilt of truly listening.

LUCIDOR: All of you? So much the more unpardonable! How could you look at me all day without shame, having so wrongly cheated me by night? Ah, but now I see it clearly and simply, your daytime plans were precisely calculated just to make sport of me. An estimable family indeed! And where now is that love of justice of your father's? And Lucinde! –

JULIE: 'And Lucinde! –' What sort of tone is this? Surely what you mean to say is, how deeply it hurts you to have to think ill of Lucinde, to have to cast Lucinde in one class with the rest of us?

LUCIDOR: I do not understand Lucinde.

JULIE: You mean, this pure, noble soul, this calm, composed being, goodness, benevolence itself, this 'woman as should be', this paragon, associates herself with such frivolous company, with a flighty sister, a spoilt child of a brother, and those various other enigmatic persons – this is incomprehensible.

LUCIDOR: Yes, indeed, this is incomprehensible.

JULIE: Then try to comprehend! Like all of us, Lucinde's hands were tied. If you could but have seen her predicament,

53

how she could hardly restrain herself from telling you everything, you would love her doubly, trebly, were not every true
love already by its very nature ten-fold, one hundred-fold
itself. And also I assure you, in the end the sport became too
long for any of us.

LUCIDOR: Then why did you not end it?

JULIE: That too can be explained. After that first speech of
yours came to father's attention, and he quickly came to
understand that there would be no objection from any of
his children to such a change, he resolved to visit your
father without delay. The importance of the business concerned him greatly; only a father can feel the respect that is
due to a father. 'He should know it first,' said mine, 'lest
later, when we are all in agreement, he should have to give a
forced and resentful consent. I know him very well; I know
how he clings to a thought, an inclination, a purpose, and
it makes me quite uneasy. Julie, his maps and his charts are
so closely connected in his thoughts that he was already
planning eventually to transfer everything here, as soon as
the day came for the young pair to settle and they would
find themselves less able to move home and position. He
was minded to devote all his vacations to us, and to whatever other kindnesses and goodness his heart intended.
He must certainly be the first to learn what sort of trick
Nature has played on us, while nothing is as yet out in the
open, nothing so far decided.' Then he made us all promise
most solemnly that we would watch over you and keep
you in check, come what may. As for how his return to us
was delayed, and the art, the toil and persistence it cost
to obtain your father's approval, that you must hear from
his own lips. Enough now, the matter is settled; Lucinde
is now yours.

And so the pair quickly left the seat where they had been; pausing on the way, talking all the while, slowly moving on again over the meadow, they reached the higher ground, and with it another well-laid roadway. The carriage came quickly up to them; and now Julie directed her neighbour's attention towards a remarkable scene. All of that machinery, on which her brother so prided himself, was now in animated movement; the wheels were carrying a multitude of people up and down, the swings were flying, poles being climbed, and there was all manner of daring swinging and springing to be seen above the heads of a countless throng. All of this had been set in movement by the young squire so that after dinner the guests might be happily entertained. 'You drive on through the lower village,' Julie called. 'The people wish me well, and they should see how well things are going for me!'

The village was deserted; the young had all already hurried to the amusement park and old men and women, roused by the post-horn, appeared at doors and windows; everywhere there were greetings, blessings, cries of 'Oh, what a lovely couple!'

JULIE: So there you have it! We would have been well matched after all; you may yet have cause for regret!

LUCIDOR: But as things are, dear sister-in-law ...

JULIE: So now I am 'dear', now that you are rid of me, is that it?

LUCIDOR: It is just a single word! But on you there is a heavy burden of responsibility; what was the meaning of that squeeze of the hand, when you knew my awful position, and you felt it too? I never saw anything in the world so utterly wicked!

JULIE: Thank God it is now atoned for, and all is forgiven. I did not want you – that is true, but *you* not wanting *me* at all – that is something no girl can forgive; the squeeze of the hand was, mark you, one for the rogue! I confess, it was more roguish itself than was fair, and I forgive myself only through forgiving you – and so let all be forgiven and forgotten. Here you have my hand.

He took it in his, and said, 'Here we are once more! Once again in our park, and now soon it will be off with us around the wide world, and no doubt back again. We shall meet again.'

They had come to the garden house. It seemed empty; the company, unsettled at finding the dinner so long delayed, had gone off for a walk. But Antoni and Lucinde now stepped forward. Julie leapt down from the carriage towards her friend, and thanked him with a heartfelt embrace, unable to hold back her tears of joy. The noble fellow's cheeks reddened, his features relaxed and opened, his eyes moistened, and out from the shell emerged a fine, imposing young man.

And so the two young couples moved back to join the company, with such sentiments as never even the loveliest of dreams could yield.

# Not too Far!

It struck ten at night, and so all was ready at the appointed hour. In the drawing room, decorated with garlands, a graceful and ample table was laid for four, with refined desserts and fancy sweetmeats arranged between flowers and glowing candles. How the children looked forward to these after-dinner delicacies! For they were to join the adult company at table; in the mean time they crept around, dressed up and masked; and as it is impossible for children to be really disfigured, they appeared the sweetest of fairy twins. The father called them to him, and they performed, in good style and with minimal assistance, the celebratory speech composed for their mother's birthday.

Time slipped by; from one quarter of an hour to the next the worthy old woman could not refrain from intensifying the impatience of our friend. Several lamps, she said, were about to go out on the staircase; she feared the lady's chosen favourite delicacies could be overdone. The children first grew naughty through boredom, then from impatience they became quite unbearable. The father kept a grip on himself, and yet his usual imperturbability was deserting him. He strained his ears, yearning for the sounds of carriages, of which indeed several rattled past without stopping; a certain vexation began to rise in him. To pass the time he demanded yet another performance from the children. But tiredness made them inattentive and distracted and inept, and they bungled their words; not a single gesture was now correct, and they over-played their parts, like actors without genuine feeling. The good man's anguish grew with every moment. It was gone a quarter to eleven. But let us hand over to him, and hear his own description of what came next:

'The clock chimed eleven; my impatience had risen to despair. Hope had given way to fear. I was afraid she might enter, flightily excuse herself with that customary ease and charm of hers, state that she was very tired, and make as if to accuse me of curbing her pleasures. Inside me everything was going round and round, and many a pain that I had endured for years now flooded back to weigh down my heart. I began to hate her. I could think of no way to conduct myself so as to receive her; the dear children, dressed up like little angels, slept peacefully on the sofa. The ground burned beneath my feet; I lost all understanding of myself, and nothing remained for me but to flee, so at least as to ride out those next moments. I hurried out to the front door, lightly and festively clad as I was. I have no idea what kind of excuse I stuttered out to the worthy old woman, but she forced an overcoat upon me and I found myself out in the street in a state I had not experienced in years. Like the young man in the grip of passion, quite lost as to where he is going, I ran up and down the streets. I would have made my way out into the open country were it not for a cold, damp wind blowing, strong and disagreeable enough to set some bounds to my displeasure.'

It will be strikingly observable in this extract that we have arrogated to ourselves the rights of the epic poet and hurled our indulgent reader all too quickly into the midst of a display of passion. Here we see an important personage in a state of domestic bewilderment, without having learnt anything further about him. Simply to throw at least a little light on the situation, we shall therefore join the worthy old woman and eavesdrop on whatever she may mutter to herself, or perhaps even cry out aloud, in her distress and confusion.

'I have long known it. I predicted it. I did not spare my lady; I often warned her, but this is stronger than she is. The master tires himself out all day with his work in the chancellery, in the town, or in the country, then in the evening he comes home to an empty house, or else to company not to his taste. She just cannot help it; if she does not constantly see people around her, if she is not always driving back and forth, if she cannot be forever dressing, undressing, changing, it is as if the very breath has gone out of her. Today, on her birthday, off she goes early into the country. Fine! In the mean time we make everything ready here. She promises solemnly to be home at nine; we are ready. The master hears the children go through the lovely poem they have learnt by heart; they are all dressed up. Lamps, lights, boiled and roasted dishes, there is nothing missing, but does she come? The master has great control over himself; he hides his impatience, but it has to break out in the end. He leaves the house so late! You can see why. But where to? I often threatened her with rival lovers – honestly, frankly. Up to now I didn't notice anything stirring in the master; one beauty has long been watching out for him, paying him attentions. Who knows what a struggle he has had so far! But now it is breaking out; this time despair is driving him out of the house late at night – despair at not seeing his good will better recognised. This time I really think all is lost. I told her more than once, she should not push things too far.'

Now let us seek out our friend again, and hear him in his own words.

'In the most respectable inn I saw light downstairs; I knocked on the window, and when the waiter looked out I asked him – he knew my voice – whether perhaps some strangers had arrived or were due to arrive. Opening the door immediately, he answered "no" to both questions, but he asked me in. In the circumstances I found it convenient to continue with the sham; I asked for a room, which he promptly gave me on the third floor, for the second floor should be kept for the expected guests. He hurried off to organise a few things; I left him to it, promising to settle the account myself. So far things had gone well, but I now sank back into my woes, picturing to myself each and every aspect of the situation, exaggerating, qualifying everything; I upbraided myself, then attempted to compose and soothe myself; the next morning, I felt, I could start all over again, and I thought how I could once more set about my daily life in the normal way. But then once again all of my resentment burst out uncontrollably; I had never thought that I could feel so wretched.'

This noble gentleman, whom we unexpectedly see here so passionately exercised over a seemingly minor event, has no doubt inspired in our readers such concern that they will wish to hear a more detailed explanation of his circumstances. We shall avail ourselves of the break that now occurs in our night-time adventure, leaving our hero to pace silently, impetuously, back and forth in the room.

We are now making the acquaintance of Odoard, as the scion of an ancient household, to whom were passed down through the generations the noblest of excellent qualities. His military-academy education endowed him with a certain gentility and ease of manner, which in combination with his most commendable mental gifts lent his comportment a quite particular charm. Through a brief period of court service he had gained considerable understanding of the ways and practices of the upper echelons; and when, by and by, through rapidly earned high favour he joined a diplomatic legation and had the opportunity to see the world and get to know foreign courts, his clarity of intellectual grasp and his fine memory, down to the minutest particulars, of what had occurred, but above all his sincerity in any kind of undertaking, very soon shone forth. His fluency in expression in a number of languages, together with an easy but unobtrusive personal manner, brought him from one step to the next; in all missions, because he was able to gain an advantage through winning the good will of people, he proved particularly skilled in settling dissensions, and indeed at satisfying both sides' interests through the judicious balancing of the matters at issue.

To make such a paradigm his own man was the intention of the First Minister. He gave him the hand of his daughter, a lady of the utmost beauty and endowed with every higher social virtue. And yet, as the flow of all human happiness will always at some time meet with a dam to restrain it, so was to be the case here too. At the princely court, Princess Sophronie was brought up as a ward; the last offshoot of her family branch, her fortune and aspirations remained quite considerable, notwithstanding that the estates and their inhabitants would pass to her uncle. In order, therefore, to obviate protracted discussion, it was desired that she be married to the young hereditary Prince – who was, in truth, far younger than she.

Odoard was suspected of feeling an inclination towards her. It was felt that he had exalted her rather too ardently in a poem, under the name of Aurora; furthermore, in a moment of incaution on her side she had countered with defiance certain teasings from her young companions, retorting that she would have had to have no eyes at all in her head if she were to be blind to such fine qualities.

Such suspicions were, admittedly, silenced by Odoard's marriage, but they continued nevertheless to be fed, and from time to time rekindled, by secret enemies.

Matters of state and inheritance, much as people tried to touch on them as little as possible, were sometimes mentioned. The Prince himself, and more so his shrewd counsellors, considered it in every way expedient to let the matter rest from now on, while the Princess's silent supporters wished to see it brought to an end, and the noble lady thereby given greater freedom, especially as the neighbouring elderly King, who was related to Sophronie and was favourably disposed towards her, still lived and had on occasion shown himself ready to use a fatherly influence on her behalf.

There arose the suspicion that, during a purely ceremonial mission, Odoard had again stirred up the business that it had been hoped to check. His enemies took advantage of the event, and his father-in-law, whom he had convinced of his innocence, had to use all of his influence to obtain for him a kind of governorship in a distant province. Here Odoard was happy, for he was able to bring all of his talents into play. Here there were necessary, useful, good, fine, important things to accomplish, and here he could make a lasting contribution without sacrificing himself, instead of risking, against his own conviction, sinking under the weight of ephemeral activities.

His wife saw matters rather differently; she was a person who could only truly exist in wider social circles, and she followed Odoard only later, and under compulsion. His be-haviour towards her could not have been more solicitous; he happily supported every surrogate for the happiness she had known thus far – excursions into the neighbouring country-side in the summer, amateur dramatics in the winter, balls, and any other activity she was minded to introduce.

He even tolerated a household companion in the form of a stranger who had installed himself some time ago, although he did not like the man at all, for with his discriminating eye for human types he firmly believed that he detected a certain falseness in him.

Of all of that we have recorded here, some part may have passed darkly and dimly through Odoard's mind at the present critical moment – and some part of it more clearly and distinctly. Suffice it to say that when we turn, after this intimate disclosure (the material of which has been communicated to us through the fine memory of our source), back to Odoard himself, we encounter him once again pacing impetuously up and down in the room and displaying, through gestures and even exclamations, his inner conflict.

'Amidst such thoughts I had been pacing impetuously up and down in the room; the waiter had brought me a cup of broth, which I sorely needed; thanks to all those painstaking preparations for the festivities, I had eaten nothing, and an excellent supper lay untouched on the table at home. That moment we heard the pleasant sound of a post-horn coming up the street. The waiter said, "He'll have come from the hills." We went to the window, and by the light of two brightly shining carriage lamps we saw a lordly carriage advancing, four-horsed, well packed. The attendants sprang off the box. "Here they are!" cried the waiter, and hurried to the door. I held him back, and impressed upon him that he should say nothing of my presence, nor divulge that anything had been ordered. He duly promised, and dashed off.

'Meanwhile I had neglected to observe who stepped out of the vehicle, and I was overcome by a new impatience; the waiter seemed to me to be far too long about bringing news. Finally I learnt from him that the guests were women – one a somewhat older, respectable-looking lady, another her junior, unbelievably gracious, and finally a maid-servant who would have charmed anyone. "The maid started," he said, "with orders, and continued with flattery, and then when I made up to her she became all gay and saucy, and that may well have been her most natural self. I very soon noticed," he went on, "their general astonishment at finding me so alert, and the house so ready to receive them – rooms lit, fires burning; they made themselves at home, and found a cold supper in the dining room; I offered them some broth, which they seemed to welcome.'"

The ladies were now seated at the table; the older one hardly ate anything, the beautiful, charming one nothing at all. The maid, whom they called Lucie, tucked in with great relish, at the same time extolling the merits of the inn, delighting in the bright candles and the fine table-linen and the china and all the utensils. She had already warmed herself by the blazing fire, and when the waiter came in again she asked him, were they then always so ready to receive guests arriving without notice at any hour of the day or night? The nifty young fellow behaved in this case like a child who, while keeping the secret itself, cannot conceal the fact that he has been given a secret to keep. To start with he gave an equivocal answer, then came nearer the truth, and finally, cornered by the maid's vivacity and badinage, confessed that a servant – no, a gentleman, had come – no, had gone – had left again – had returned – and he finally let slip that the gentleman was in fact upstairs and was anxiously walking up and down. The young lady leapt up, as did the others after her: 'It must be an old gentleman!' she cried excitedly. The waiter assured them it was not; he was young. Now they again doubted his word, but he swore by what he had said. Their confusion and unease grew. It could only be her uncle, asserted the beautiful lady, but the older woman answered that this would be quite out of character with him. But, countered the other firmly, nobody but her uncle could have known that they would turn up here at such an hour. The waiter repeatedly swore that it was a young, vigorous, attractive man. Against this Lucie vowed it must be the uncle: this rascal, the waiter, was not to be believed – he had already been contradicting himself for half an hour.

After all of this the waiter was forced to go upstairs and earnestly beg the gentleman to come down quickly – threatening that the ladies would otherwise come up themselves and thank him in person. 'This is such an endless mess!' continued the waiter. 'I just cannot understand why you hesitate! Let them see you; they say you are an old uncle whom they passionately long to embrace again. Do go down, I beg you! Are these not the very persons you were expecting? Don't be so wilful, turning your back on such a charming adventure; she is really worth seeing, and hearing, that young beautiful one, and they are the most respectable of people. Now go down, hurry, or else they'll burst in on you, right here into the room.'

Passion engenders passion. Unsettled as he was, Odoard longed for something different, something new. He went down, hoping to account for himself, to clarify his behaviour in cheerful conversation with these new arrivals, and to hear something of other people's affairs and distract himself; and yet it somehow seemed to him that this was a more familiar, threatening situation that now awaited him. He was before the door; the ladies thought they heard the uncle's steps, and ran to greet him. In he stepped. What a meeting! What a spectacle! The young beauty let forth a cry, and threw herself around the neck of the older woman. Our friend, recognising them both, recoiled, then felt himself driven forward, lying at her feet, touching her hand, which he just as quickly released again with the most discreet kiss. On his lips faded the syllables 'Au-ro-ra'.

Turning our eyes once again to the house of our friend, there we find some quite peculiar circumstances. The worthy old woman had no idea what to do, or not to do. She kept the lamps alight in the hall and on the steps; she had taken the food off the fire, some of it now irretrievably spoilt. The young chambermaid had stayed with the sleeping children and guarded the numerous candles in their rooms; as she moved around she was as gentle and patient as the older woman was ill-humoured. At last the carriage rolled up. The lady stepped out and was informed that her husband had been called away a few hours before. As she climbed the steps she appeared to take no notice of the festive lighting. The old woman now learnt from the servant that they had met with an accident on the way and the carriage had been thrown into a ditch, with all the many consequences.

The lady entered the room. 'What kind of masquerade have we here?' she inquired, pointing to the children. 'It would have given you much pleasure,' answered the maid, 'if you had come a few hours earlier.' The children were shaken out of their sleep; they leapt up, and on seeing their mother before them they began the speech that they had learnt by heart. They continued for a while, with embarrassment on both sides; then, having no one to encourage or prompt, they broke down completely, and the little dears were sent back to bed with a few hugs. The lady, finding herself alone, threw herself upon the sofa and broke into bitter tears.

But now once again it is necessary to give some further details, about both the lady herself and this apparently most ill-starred country celebration. Albertine was one of those women to whom people have little to say when alone with them, but whom they are very happy to meet in wider company, for there they appear as true adornments of the whole party, as agents of instant revival whenever a lull occurs. Their charm is of the kind that requires some space to express itself and work its effect comfortably; their success depends on having a larger public, as they need an element to support them and to require them to exert their charm. When alone with someone, they hardly know how to behave at all.

The household companion had gained and sustained her favour purely through knowing how to set in train one diversion after another and keep a happy, if not large, circle going. When the dramatic roles were assigned he tended to choose the part of the tender father, and he knew how to use a demeanour of respectability and gravity to upstage the first, second and third younger gallants of the piece.

Florine, the owner of a considerable neighbouring estate, spent the winters in town; she was much beholden to Odoard, whose arrangements in the region's economy had, by accident but also by good fortune, greatly advantaged her holdings. In consequence the prospect was offered of significantly increasing their profitability. Florine's summers were spent on the estate, which she made the setting for a great variety of respectable recreations. Birthdays above all were never neglected, and parties of every description were arranged.

Florine was a vivacious, playful soul, apparently unattached and not seeking or wanting any particular alliance. An enthusiastic dancer, she appreciated men only inasmuch as they could keep time as they moved. Ever the lively social creature, she had no patience at all with those who even for one moment looked on silently and appeared lost in thought. Furthermore she winningly took the part of the cheerful *jeune*, essential in any play or opera; consequently there was never any competitiveness between her and Albertine, who always took the more respectable roles.

With a view to celebrating the forthcoming birthday in good company, the very best of guests had been invited from the town and the surrounding country. The dancing had already begun straight after breakfast, and continued after dinner. The party was long drawn out; they left too late, and were suddenly surprised and overcome by night on a poor road made twice as bad by being at the time under repair. The coachman blundered, and the carriage went into a ditch. Our beautiful lady, Florine and the household companion found themselves in a dreadful tangle together; the companion managed to wriggle out quickly and, leaning over the carriage, cried, 'Florine, where are you?' Albertine thought she was dreaming; he thrust in his arms and hauled out, in a faint, Florine, who was lying on top. He earnestly tended her and finally carried her in his strong arms up along the road which now came back into view. Albertine was still held trapped in the carriage; the coachman and the servant helped her out. Supported by the latter, she tried to walk. The path was rough, hardly suitable for dancing shoes; though helped along by the young lad, she stumbled every moment. But in her mind everything seemed even more wild, more desolate; she did not know, could not comprehend, what had happened.

When she entered the inn and saw Florine lying on the bed in that little room, with the landlady and Lelio attending to her, then she was quite convinced of her misfortune. A secret liaison between him – her faithless companion – and her treacherous friend was revealed in the briefest instant as she saw her friend open her eyes, throw her arms around the companion in the ecstasy of a newly reawakened, tenderest claim to possession, her dark eyes shining once more, her pale cheeks again suddenly graced with new glow. She really did seem younger, charming, never lovelier.

Albertine stood and stared, alone, hardly noticed. The others recovered and collected themselves. But the damage was done; they were forced to sit together again in that carriage, and scarcely even in Hell itself could souls so hateful to one another be so closely crammed together – the betrayed with their own betrayers.

Johann Wolfgang von Goethe was born in Frankfurt am Main in 1749 to Johann Caspar Goethe, an Imperial Councillor, and Katherine Elizabeth Textor, the daughter of the mayor of Frankfurt. In 1765 he was sent, against his wishes, to Leipzig to study Law. An unhappy affair inspired his first play, *Caprice*, which appeared in 1767. Then followed a period of illness, during which time he published some lyric poems. He eventually completed his studies in Strasbourg in 1771, and went on to practise Law.

Goethe's first novel, *Die Leiden des jungen Werthers* [*The Sorrows of Young Werther*], was published in 1774. Partly autobiographical, it was given a sensational reception throughout Europe, and led to Goethe's recognition as a leading figure in the *Sturm und Drang* movement. The following year he was invited to the Court of the Duke of Weimar, where he remained for much of his life, occupying various government positions. In 1786 he travelled to Italy, a period of his life he later recounted in *Die italienische Reise* [*Italian Journey*] (1816–17). His stay there instilled in him a passion for the classical ideal, and a move away from his earlier *Sturm und Drang* tendencies. The works that followed – *Iphigenie auf Tauris* (1787), *Egmont* (1788), and *Torquato Tasso* (1789) among them – clearly demonstrate this new influence.

From 1796 Goethe was occupied by his Wilhelm Meister series. The first instalment, *Wilhelm Meisters Lehrjahre* [*The Apprenticeship of Wilhelm Meister*] (1796), soon became the prototype for the German *Bildungsroman*. The series was completed in 1829 with *Wilhelm Meisters Wanderjahre* [*Wilhelm Meister's Journeyman Years*]. Goethe is, however, probably best remembered for his play, *Faust*, which was based on the popular Renaissance legend of a famous German alchemist who supposedly sold his soul to the devil for insight into the secret laws of nature. The legend was first printed in 1587 as a popular chapbook entitled *Historia von D. Johann Fausten*, on which Christopher Marlowe's well-known play, *Dr Faustus*, was based. The first part of Goethe's *Faust* appeared in 1808; the second shortly after his death in 1832. He was buried in the same mausoleum as Friedrich von Schiller, who had died a quarter of a century earlier.

Jonathan Katz is a linguist, musician and musicologist now teaching at Westminster School, London. Formerly he was a Research Fellow of Wolfson College, Oxford, and he has held visiting posts at Princeton and Oxford Universities. His publications include translations from German and Italian and articles on Greek and Latin and Indian Classical literature.

Andrew Piper is an Assistant Professor in the Department of German Studies and an Associate Member of the Department of Art History and Communication Studies at McGill University in Canada. He is the author of *Dreaming in Books: The Making of the Bibliographic Imagination in the Romantic Age* (Chicago 2009) and a biography of Goethe that appeared as part of Hesperus' Brief Lives series. His previous translation of Goethe's work, *The Man of Fifty*, also appeared with Hesperus. He is currently at work on a project on Goethe, print and autobiography entitled, *The Medium of Myself*.